TROUBLES ON THE HORIZON
Surviving Y2K

by
Jerry W. Rockett

Writers Club Press
San Jose · New York · Lincoln · Shanghai

ISBN: 1-893652-32-7

This book was published using the on-line/on-demand
publishing services of Writers Club Press, an imprint of
iUniverse, Inc.

iUniverse.com, Inc.
620 North 48th Street
Suite 201
Lincoln NE 68504-3467
www.iuniverse.com

URL: http://www.writersclub.com

ACKNOWLEDGMENTS

<u>Bera Izora Black Rockett,</u> a storyteller of family events from her childhood, my father's family, and many, many stories about her youth and early adulthood. Because of her, my siblings and I have a sense of family, a sense of history as it relates to the two halves of our parentage. I was delighted as a child to hear her tell of daily events of her school days. To know from her stories the various family groups to which we were related and how through multiple marriages , these people were part of my extended family. Only recently have I realized what influence her free flowing storytelling would have upon my own style of storytelling. For my early beginnings as a listener, until this time as a serious writer, I give her honor and credit, my mother.

<u>Ann Paine,</u> a very dear friend from Jackson, Mississippi. Ann is a talented writer in her own right and has encouraged me to tell this story. Willow, as I have nicknamed her because of her magical poems about the willow, saw in my attempts at prose promises that needed expanding and exercising. Using her experience as a gifted child instructor, she instructed me but most of all, she believed in my ability and encouraged me to see the project to its completion.

<u>Prof. E. Young</u>, long gone from walking this earth but still much alive, at least in my memory. Miss Young was my freshman year English professor and would not accept less than my best,

in my style. She was the first to recognize that I had some talent but lacked the exposure to literature so needed for becoming a credible writer. She insisted I learn to love reading. Since those early college days, nearly each time I pick up another book to read, I think of Miss Young and whisper a silent thank you. Through Miss Young's encouragement to learn to love reading, I have traveled the world and the universe. I still thank Miss Young for this gift.

James E. Bagley, not only a very dear friend but my first proof-reader and critic. Jimmy is a Doctor of Law and has a great command of the English language. The greatest compliment from him was when he told me he liked my style of writing, and though he would have phrased things differently, he graciously accepted mine without red lining the entire manuscript. For his encouragement, friendship and acceptance, I offer my thanks.

Chapter 1

Y2K-2000

My name is Thomas Sparks, the year is 2002, early fall. I have just moved into my hideaway cave. After almost three years of painstaking planning, yet I am a little shocked, and saddened. Profoundly awed by the correctness of my earlier prediction of the world going mad as the result of the year 2000 computer problems. Clearly I had prepared for this event as if I alone could see it's inevitable coming.

Three years ago, who would have thought the world would plunge itself into an ever expanding financial chaos? Who could have seen or even dreamed that two great industrial nations would be among the first victims. Russia, an industrial giant and world leader, failed both politically and economically during the early days of the year 2000. Japan was showing signs of economic failure even as far back as 1998, but no one really believed it would fail. It seemed to have only days, but each day it held on precariously. Yet I had seen it, predicted it in writings and conversations with whomever would listen. Most people didn't understand what was involved with the year 2000 (later referred to as the Y2K problem) problem and computers.

In my earlier evaluations of the impact to world economy, I had determined that the major player's of the world economy would have addressed the issue and resolved the potential problem. The lesser developed countries, or third world countries, would be the early and only victims. The reasoning had been that they were the least prepared to deal with the problem, therefore, least prepared to cope with the traumas of Y2K. Since they could not correct nor prevent the resulting associated problems, they would fail, then their trading partner neighbors, their suppliers and a small trickle effecting the more effluent industrialized nations. Nothing to really worry about.

I feel badly about what is happening. I also feel a little guilty. You see, I served on the committee of the United States Government which first identified and defined the data dictionary for computer and programming language usage. This data dictionary had been accepted as the standard for data field names and lengths. Thus was triggered the era of shorthand representation of the century date, dropping the 19 to save expensive data storage space. Of course, this was not the only data field shortened.

The world of data processing accepted this short hand coding system with almost a sigh of relief. Everyone knew how expensive space was and could not see that this particular data item was of any critical significance, certainly not then. Even had the thought crossed our minds, we would surely have resolved the problem at some more convenient time.

I suspect that even the average member of society of today does not understand what our committee's recommendations meant to their future, today. At first it was to save very valuable memory space. Algorithms using the YY (year code) could easily assume the century code of 19. Coding for calculations of taxes, payroll, bond maturity, amortization charts, and so many more accounting type transactions worked so smoothly. Then the cost of changing back to full representation of the century-year date seemed prohibitive. Why bother anyway, everything was working satisfactorily? More and more institutions began using this successful shorthand of representation of data. The institutions of military, financial, industrial control systems, insurance, educational, medical and of course, government were using its advantages.

No one foresaw that as the date rolled over to January 01, 2000, that firmware controlling elevators in a high rise apartment would cease to function, that people would be stranded. Nor that air traffic controllers would lose their primary tool, the computer, to safely conduct the landing and take off of thousands of planes around the world. That almost anything controlled by a computer or a computer clock chip could be effected by not having reconciled the impact of omitting the century designation in the year field. Train traffic would stall, street lights and medical instruments would cease functioning properly, vaults opening or not, security systems failing and what about the military functions, how far would it reach?

In 1998, I was winding down a thirty year career in which I had been engaged in data processing. So many people were talking about the potential disaster of the year 2000 (Y2K). It was my task to determine its possible negative or disruptive effect upon my employer's facilities and it's business welfare. We were among the lucky ones and could expect only minor adjustments or corrective action in order to be in compliance. Even so, the media and associates kept me reminded of the impending threat to the world as a whole.

I soon became obsessed with the problem. Using the Internet, I could monitor the progress of prevention being applied throughout the world, especially in the industrialized nations. Gradually, a strong impression took hold which was that the less developed nations lacked the financial and manpower resources to cope with the problem. Like many others, I accepted the calculated risk their failure would have on the financial and stable condition of the major players in the world economy. The majors would be in compliance and a few minor countries would fail.

3

It was a time when so much of our attention was being drawn toward an embarrassed president. We were being divided over this issue and had a tendency to ignore the world situation, financially. We had all witnessed the rise and fall of the stock markets, large nations having temporary difficulties but always in the past, in most of our memories, our government had performed miracles and we would move on to bigger and better things in the new millennium, hey the president had promised that.

Early warnings were being ignored. Japan's economy was on the brink of collapse. Russia had presidential problems and still could not decide to remain a democracy or return to communism. Asia as a whole was having financial difficulties, even to the extent of affecting our world trade in areas that greatly effected our farmers and some manufacturing companies. Of course, Iraq kept poking up its threatening head, possibly leading to another military conflict.

Lay offs from major industries were being reported almost daily. Mergers of great magnitude were being performed to save cost of doing business. Countries in areas of the world critical to world peace were developing the atomic bomb, or so it was being reported. A world in trouble before the critical date would only heighten the potential chaos that Y2K implied.

But in 2002, I moved from my farm cottage to this secret cave.

Chapter 2

NEW HOME

In the fall of 1998, I was able to purchase an old homestead site near the community of Eureka Springs which is in the NW corner of Arkansas. There were no structures left on the place but it did have the remains of an old apple orchard and a scattering of pear, peach and plum. In addition, it had what looked like the remains of an old garden plot.

I sat up my motor home in a nice shady spot, arranged for electrical service and contacted a well driller. In the mean time I had to use bottled water until I could find a source of water on the property. Of course, the old well used by the homesteaders years ago was no good and had so much trash which had been thrown into it I was leery of using it. I had also been told that the property had a year round spring. That would have to be found later. Right now what I needed was to decide where to build the house.

In 1990, I had contracted to have a modernized Acadian house built. I had put in a large amount of sweat equity in its construction and had originally designed the house. It was the most liveable house in which I had ever lived. Here, I wanted something with the same feel of comfort and livability, a log cabin, and cottage all wrapped up in one package. So my plans were to have it raised off the ground, nice front porch facing a lovely view and very open inside with a large kitchen, fireplace and lots of windows. It had to be structurally simple, and lend itself to timber construction. I had prepared basic drawings and then took these to an architect friend of mine. After some modifications, the plans were drawn up and now to do the work.

I had purchased a one man sawmill, of the circular type, in the summer of 1995. Originally, my plans were to fell the trees from my own property, cut the timbers and other wood plankings I would need and enjoy building my house. The property I owned just did not have the volume nor tree sizes needed to do this without destroying too much of its overall beauty. So after some searching, I located a hauler that could provide me with logs. The timbers for the main wall construction were to be 4 inches by 8 inches laid on top of each other on the 8 inch side. So the logs had to have a certain dimension to maximize the resulting cut timber pieces. This was arranged with the hauler and my saw mill days began in earnest.

A one man saw mill of my type is not nearly so difficult as some I have seen, and worked. Most band type sawmills take two men, otherwise that one man works too hard. Of course, the vendor never tells you that. My mill came from a manufactory outside Portland, Oregon and had been built to operate in very remote surroundings. It is truly the most "one man" saw mill I have seen in operation.

Contrary to what most people believe, green lumber can be used very successfully in constructing a house. Some woods are better than others but all will experience some shrinkage and possibly warping. If these things are taken into consideration at the onset of your project, very little rework will be required. The one thing I was concerned with was allowing proper ventilation between one timber and the one on top. I solved this problem by placing quarter inch dowels between them and chalking in between later. Another thing that helped resolve this problem was the time lapse. By the time I cut all the timbers and other pieces of wood I needed to construct the house, considerable drying had occurred.

Well, I found the spot on the property that would provide a good view, and had some trees close enough to provide shade. It had a gentle slope to the back of the house, and this would provide good drainage. After laying out the foundation, locating the footing spots, the hard work began. Now the dirt of the NW corner of Arkansas is not hard dirt but the stones and rocks it covers ARE. Using a pick and shovel, I dug the necessary space for a concrete footing and poured concrete and set reinforcement bars in place. I used native stones and mortar to build up the piers. After these had time to cure, I laboriously poured concrete in the hollow left from their construction. With the r-bars and concrete, the piers would be there long after the wood house decayed.

Building a house in this manner is not terribly hard but slow. One man can do most of the work, but an extra set of hands are a very welcome pleasure, occasionally. Doing the rafter work, setting windows and moving the various fixture for the house to their proper place, you really do need extra hands. Wall construction, plumbing, electrical work and roofing can be done alone if need be. Doing it almost by myself, it took me six months to complete the shell of the house, install the prefab-fireplace, install all the fixtures and have the air conditioner and heating systems installed.

Having completed so much, I decided to move into the house and do the finish work one room at a time. Believe me, this was a big mistake. I had not realized how time consuming finish work would be and then having to work around furniture and equipment just added to the burden. I could have finished this phase of the project two months sooner had I just kept myself in the motor home.

After one year of construction on the house, while building raised garden beds, retaining walls for the spring I found and many other chores, the house was completed. The view is marvelous, the house or cottage is very comfortable, the fireplace is a joy and my pride of accomplishment soars with the eagles. I am home.

Chapter 3

TROUBLED TIMES

The news I heard was not good. During the long year of house construction, I didn't have a lot of time to listen to the news. Yet, I could not or would not completely isolate myself. I still had some concern about the Y2K thing and hoped that my conclusions were in error.

Here it is late 1999 and still the media is talking about getting prepared for the century change. Some are making predictions similar to my conclusions but few are heeding them. More reports of governments having to take over troubled banks, attempts to shore up the economy of this country or that country. The Arab countries still not at rest, still threatening. And worst of all, my own country was still in turmoil over president Clinton.

One of the nice things that people ought to realize is that just because a certain person comes from a state, the good or bad they represent is not indicative of the good or bad of that state or her people. Arkansas did not form the value system or personality of the person we know as president Clinton. The people, as a whole, in this state are of the highest caliber and I feel privileged to be accepted by them and to feel a part of them.

Back to the news, I don't like to hear that Brazil and Mexico are still having economic problems. Asia is not recovering as fast as had been previously predicted. These situations were beginning to tell on the United States' economy. They represented our greatest export outlets and if they could not buy, we could not sell. Exporters were slowing down on purchases, factories were cutting down on production and laying off workers and these events all effected the retail merchants in hometown America. It has always been hard to spend hard earned cash when so little of it is available.

One of the most troubling events being reported was the continued failure of the family farm and the small business operations. These have been the back bone of our economy for as long as our nation has existed. Now, it seemed that all the national support was going to the larger operations, relief was going to the corporations and the little guy was being squeezed out. Squeezed out through lack of government support, shackled by too stringent regulations and voluminous paper work. Even the taxing system seem to favor the larger businesses over the small businesses and especially the small farmer. The well-to-do's did and the rest of us didn't.

I ask myself what would happen to our country when the small man can no longer afford to operate a business. When this small business can no longer compete fairly with the large corporations. What happens to our country when we lose the entrepreneurial spirit that has sustained our country, our economy for all these years. Instead of our government stymieing this spirit by indifference, it ought to be rejoicing for its presence and passing laws in support. They will, finally, when it is too late. I hate to sound cynical, but history predicts this on the part of our national leaders, our law makers. They will see the handwriting on the wall after the wall begins to crumble.

The end-timers were having a field day, with their gloom and doom prophesies. Everything that happened confirmed to them that the End Times were upon us. Now as I understand the meaning, End Times truly begins with the promised return of the Messiah, Jesus the Christ to Christians, was prophesied in many of the

Old Testament books as well as Revelation of the New Testament. It was mentioned in several of the New Testament books but primarily Revelation. So if I read these accounts correctly, we have been in the period proceeding the End Times since the resurrection of Jesus. I also understand that many prophecies must be fulfilled before the actual End Times are here and to my knowledge all of these have not occurred. I will have to do a little more research on the subject since so many religious people are convinced we are in them.

Whether End Times or Bad Times, lest I fall in the same mold, I had best make stronger efforts to be prepared.

Chapter 4

ROOT CELLAR

At first I called it my refuge cave but it is not really for refuge but it is a cave. It is basically a cave modified for use as a root cellar. In it is stored provisions that should last at least one calender year.

In late 1998, I fulfilled a dream which was one day retiring to the NW corner of Arkansas. Over the years I had obviously modified my wishes as to the type of space I wanted or needed. As the year 2000 came nearer, I was able to solidify my needs, thereby determining what was important and what was not, under the impending world circumstances.

I acquired woodland acreage, very isolated, which is almost entirely surrounded by government lands. The advantage of this is very apparent by its enhancement of isolation. The property backs up to bluffs. Issuing from the base of these bluffs is a year round spring which flows through the NE corner of the property. I have been able to dam this flow, creating a very small pond. Of course, in an emergency, this water source could be utilized for drinking and cooking. I had it checked by the state health department for potability and it was very okay.

While exploring the property where I would soon build my home, I came upon what appeared to be the opening of a cave. I marked the spot for further exploration at a much more convenient time. After several months, with flashlight in hand, I squeezed through a very small vertical opening. It was a cave, about the size of a single car detached garage, or ten foot by twelve foot and with about a fifteen foot headroom.

I am always surprised how cool a cave can be, this one staying at near a 20 to 25 degrees difference from the temperature outside. It felt humid inside and I hoped this would be true year around. My very first thought was to convert it into a storm shelter. The NW corner of Arkansas is very subject to tornadoes and forms the south eastern edge of the tornado belt. I suppose that is one of the reasons I had often referred to it as my refuge cave, refuge from the storms. The title still fits somewhat in view of the pending world crisis. My priorities were such that modifying it to serve as a root cellar overruled any further consideration of other usage, even a refuge from storms.

The storage of perishables in a root cellar requires the proper harvest of the products, a humid and cool environment, good air circulation, and protection from scavengers. This cave could have all these features, with very little effort. I took measurements and these were duplicated on paper. What I wanted was to take advantage of the coolness, humidity and weather protection the cave offered. One noticeable need was for the expansion of the entry.

The cave opening, once expanded, would be the only needed construction, other than the shelves. There was no reason to wall in the inside, since man has been using dugout root cellars for eons of time. These natural cave walls would serve the same purpose. I was not sure if air circulated deeper within the cave. It was not obvious that it extended further into the mountain side ultimately finding an air passage to the outside. So when I enclosed the opening for access and protection from intrusion of vermin, I built air slots, screened over at the bottom, and air slots at the very top, also screened over.

The floor would be leveled with sand thus providing a smoother walking surface. Having a dirt floor (sand in this case) aided in the availability of humidity and if necessary, to raise the humidity, I could moisten the sand.

The door was provided with a facing of hardware cloth and opened inward into the room space. Storage bins or shelves were constructed using almost all the available space, rising up to twelve feet in the air. Some bins were solid and others were slatted or bottomed with hardware cloth. Different products have different air circulation requirements. One thing I did remember to do was to use treated lumber for all construction components.

I was amazed at the different temperature variations from floor to ceiling and from front to back. Maybe only 5 degrees at times but with the insulated enclosure wall and door, this stilled seemed a lot. I was also amazed at those food items that could be stored. I had almost two years of experience to fall back on and this with what I could learn from the Internet, I had learn to grow those foods that best stored well in a root cellar.

Most of the leafy winter plants I could grow well into the Winter and only stored the last harvest of these for use into the Spring. Leeks, celery, horseradish, along with the carrots, beets and turnips I stored as close to the floor as possible. These like a very high humidity to remain fresh, plus it was always cooler at the bottom.

Next in line, at a slightly higher level of shelves were stored the potatoes, fresh cabbages, endive and with apples, and pears being stored above the potatoes. I had read that about the apples and pears somewhere, and it seemed to work. Higher up on shelves then came cucumbers and sweet peppers and when I could get them or raise them were cantaloupes and watermelons. These last two items were not of high priority. Slightly ripe tomatoes store will with good air circulation, however I would can most of these when ripe, using glass jars. Platted garlic was hung on nails from shelves, and red onions were stored on hardware cloth bottomed shelves. You never want the chore of cleaning up spoiled onions or potatoes, oh the smell. Dried hot peppers were sewn together and hung like garlic. Winter squash and pumpkins were added to the larder when these two products were in abundance and space allowed. All root plants were packed in sawdust and all vegetables were covered with burlap.

One of the best uses of a root cellar is for the storage of canned foods. Special shelves were constructed to carry their weight in a back section of the cellar. One thing I had to learn the hard way was to use artificial light while in the root cellar. If I need fresh food or canned items, I used a flashlight. I found out that some lamp fuels, such as kerosene used in lanterns, produce ethylene, which is a fruit ripener. This I did not want to happen. The other thing I learned early was the axiom that 'one bad apple will spoil the bushel' is true. This applies to potatoes, and onions as well.

Chapter 5

MORE BAD NEWS

It is late 1999, I have been listening and viewing the news on my television. I can tell you, it was not encouraging. A new record was set in 1998 for the number of workers laid off from their jobs. This happened in one of the most progressive of economies. Now, in this year of 1999, I have heard of new layoffs and about an economy reeling from news of disasters to the farmers, mining companies failing and manufacturing companies closing or downsizing. The unemployment figures are climbing and the Y2K problem is still looming in the background. What news this will generate as the clock ticks twelve midnight on December 31, 1999, no one really knows.

President Clinton survived the ordeal of being impeached, and then not censured by the senate. His arrogance in light of this, infuriated many, caused others to rally to his defense. Neither reaction could help him recover to his former glory or aid him in recovering his ability to lead. Even other world leaders questioned his motives and were slow in responding to world crises if he suggested an approach. His conduct of 1998 had taken their toll, and the price he ultimately had to pay was proving to be beyond his grasp.

As the news of more lay offs were reported, as the economy slowed, as more farmers failed, mines closed and plants downsized, President Clinton's popularity was beginning to slide. Even the continued support of Mrs. Clinton, Vice President Gore and Democratic leaders could not stem the tide of descent from former supporters. The American public was frightened. They feared to travel abroad due to Iraq's announced hatred for Americans and the resulting terrorist acts against tourist. They feared for the slowly but assuredly crumbling economy.

Our economy had been the strongest of all for so long, Americans had gotten use to a bullish environment. We had been a nation who led, and others listened when our leader spoke. The whole wanted this charismatic status to remain, or at least recover. When this did not appear to be happening, fingers began to point at the most vocal and obviously deserving scapegoat, the President of the United States. When a people get disenchanted with a leader, regardless of his past glory, the disenchantment accelerates like an avalanche of snow , nothing will stop it until it has run its course. Late 1999, we were hearing the rumbles of our impending avalanche.

The religious fanatics were not helping or making matters any better. With their dooms day predictions and the day of judgement being close at hand, they were beginning to be listened to. The uninformed were near panic not remembering how these same dooms day types had predicted the end of the world as we know it when 1900 rolled around, or when our nation entered the First World War. Of course, it was a different person's voice, but just as loud and just as wrong. Nor, did they remember those that declared the end when our nation entered the Second World War, or those that claimed that Adolph Hitler was obviously the predicted Anti-Christ.

Now, with economic failure being more prevalent, and of course, the beginning of a new millennium, they have started again. Out of desperation, many were listening and reacting. New and bigger religious cults were springing up every where. The tried and true denominational churches were generally failing, for as a whole, they played down these dooms day predictions. Theirs were not the soothing words that quieted the worried mind as they had for centuries.

The fanatics were drawing people into communes where foods, supplies, ammunition, water and clothing were being, at enormous rates, stockpiled. They were preparing to do battle with the Devil and his followers or any one else who did not believe their way. They found ready and willing followers from the ranks of racial isolationist, militant groups who opposed the principles of the federal government, those who supported the theme of A superior race of man, and of course, the naive and uninformed in a scriptural context.

This trend toward narrow mindedness of religious fanaticism frightened me more than the impending financial disruption of the world economy, which I suspected was coming. It was like the return of the days of Martin Luther, when confronted with the narrow religious dogma of a church in control of most of the civilized world. Luther believed that the common man had the right, if not the obligation, to interpret the scripture for himself. He did not have to be a puppet and only know what the priest said was truth. He had the right to determine his own fate by accepting or rejecting the Holy Scripture on his own. The resulting reformation freed thousands upon thousands from religious bondage and brought into being what we call the protestant church(s).

These dooms day fanatics are trying to have a type of reversal of reformation, and place thousands upon thousands back in the control of a narrow religious dogma, a dogma of their creation. Brainwashing those that had chosen not to be informed or refused to exercise the freedom brought about at great cost by Martin Luther and his followers in the 16th century. They were like cattle being led to the slaughter under the guise of escaping the unescapable.

I personally believe very strongly the prophecies of the Christian's Holy Bible. I believe there is a day of reckoning for all men. I also believe that a man of average intelligence can read these scriptures, compare the prophecies of these scriptures with modern day events and get some reasonable inkling of where we are in time as related to the prophesied happenings. We can find evidence that verifies the prophesy of the Jews being scattered throughout the world. We can pin point when the prophesy of the Jews returning to their own land happened. So it would seem to me, that the same intelligent mind could see or determine, that certain happening have not occurred and the prophesy which predicted this event just has not been fulfilled.

For the last year, I have been preparing for a very bad world economic failure. It is my conviction that our society will not be as peaceful as was found during the so called "Great Depression". I have observed during my sixty years plus the breakdown of the moral fiber of our society. It is evident when men flaunt their sexual taste for all to know, that many would take from others to satisfy their own dependent need for drugs, and others would promise vengeance against those who acted contrary to their wishes. Why should I believe I am safe from the same people who will drive by and indiscriminately fire shots at an innocent bystander. There is nothing I have seen lately that should convince me, that should circumstances of economy sink, approximating those circumstances of the depression of the '30's, that my neighbor will not try to take what I have if he and his family are without. When I say neighbor, I don't just mean those next door exclusively, but include any that have the need and can find me.

I believe in the goodness of man. I would like to believe that the world economy will survive or recover quickly enough that the worst of man has no chance to rise to the top. A rational man will not steal from me, but when a man sees his children starving or dying for lack of food, many will become irrational. While I am believing and hoping for the best, I am preparing as if the worst were a certainty. I hope the best wins out.

I detest the idea that I would be considered among the dooms day sayers. My intent is to arouse the thinking mind to review the world with a clear informed mind and place credence as they see fit. I realize that all the world cannot nor should not escape unto the hills, so to speak, and become isolationist. I had planned long and hard for the day I could return to the part of the world I most enjoyed. I have prepared for the foreboding events, as I saw them, and used what I had and have available to me.

I didn't purchase this piece of property just because it had two caves that could work in the scheme of things. I didn't know it had a year round spring. I wanted the tranquility I have found here. I sought the solitude, the beauty and the isolation so I could pursue an outlet for some of my passion for woodcraft, gardening, fishing, and even writing.

In this book, I have written about survival tactics or projects. These may suggest other things you might consider doing that better fits into your situation. The projects I have done are things I would have done even if very bad times were not on the way. I have used raised beds for years. I have composted for as long as I have gardened. It is just the circumstances of the impending disruption of world affairs, even if temporary, that has spurred me to a quicker realization of projects dreamed and planned for. Each of us must prepare for our future in our own way, using those skills and talents and means at our disposal.

Chapter 6

RAISED BEDS

During the house construction, I began to consider the construction of raised beds for the garden. Now this was one area of gardening and country living in which I had many years of experience. The one area that could be considered new was the building material I would be using for the wall construction of the raised beds.

In the NW corner of Arkansas, there is never a scarcity of available building material, as long as you want to use stones or rocks. Over the years I have used treated lumber, old cross ties, rough green lumber and tree trunks and landscape timbers. Treated lumber was the best of those but I expect excellent results from stones.

My raised beds around the resident area are 4 foot by 8, 10, or 12 foot in length, depending on their usage. Those around the root cellar are different and I will tell you about them later. So the building of stone walls that are no higher than 12 inches are much like laying brick. You use mortar between adjoining surfaces, hoping to get about a one half inch layer of mortar. I tried to use about 6 inch width stones, 3 inch in thickness and as long as I could physically handle. Most were no longer than 8 inches. This gives a very stable wall in which to hold your soil mix.

I space the beds about 3 foot apart and run them in lengths for as long as the grounds will allow or as I desire. No single bed is longer than 12 foot, and allowing 3 foot of path space, if I desire, I can have two 12 foot beds taking a length of 27 foot, or add another bed and walk path.

The advantage of raised beds over conventional row gardening is varied. One, you control the garden soil mix. Two, you have less compaction in raised beds since you nor your equipment are treading on the soil mix. Three, weed control and cultivation is easier due to the tilt of the soil and ease of seeing and reaching the weeds. Four, raised beds allow the grower to plant in a greater concentration of plants to space ratio. This last allows a greater harvest per square foot of garden space. One thing that is common between the row garden and the raised bed garden is the greater ease of insect control and plant rotation for disease control.

One of the easiest bed soils I have ever built (mixed) started with loads of horse manure/sawdust, cow manure/hay loads, dirt from a lagoon which received the refuge from washing sugar cane prior to the cane being processed for sugar and syrup. Now this soil was extra rich in phosphorous used extensively in the sugar cane fields. There is always a certain amount of soil that sticks to the stalks, then after the cut cane has its leaves burned, there is always some ash residue. The ashes have potash in it and all this ends up in the lagoons, which periodically has to be dredged. This is where I get the lagoon soil.

The soil resulting from this mixture was the best I had and have ever mixed. It seemed to get better as it aged a little and by the time I had to leave it behind, it turned out to be one of the finest earthworm beds I had ever had. So, for my new constructed raised beds, I wanted to duplicate as much of the above as possible.

I found a source for hardwood sawdust, and the owner would let me have as many loads as I wanted, just for the price of the loader operator's time. This was very cheap. The second raw material I wanted and needed was manure. In this I was very lucky, living in the NW corner of Arkansas. There are hundreds of chicken farms close by in this neck of the woods so I just had to make the proper arrangements.

Chicken manure is highly desirable for spreading on pasture lands due to its high content of nitrogen. Now the sawdust is high in carbon. The bacteria (aerobic) needed to break this down to soil needs about a 30 carbon source to 1 nitrogen source mix. So this meant heavy on the sawdust and light on the nitrogen. If you give bacteria and other microorganisms the proper environment, they will multiply to an astronomical number in a matter of days.

One major difference in using chicken manure over even aged horse or cattle manure is it is considered a very hot manure. Meaning that when in association with the right food source (carbon) bacteria will multiple so rapidly, convert this raw material so rapidly the mix as a whole will reach temperatures of around 160 degrees. At this stage, it is going through the same cycle as you would expect in a compost pile. The only way I know to curb this heat cycle is to dilute the chicken manure with what is called cold manures like aged cow manure or put it into a liquid state and pour the liquid only onto the bed material. I used chicken manure and let it go through the heat cycle before planting because it was more abundant and the heat will kill weed seeds that might be in the mix as a whole.

Over the years I have added top dressing of compost, newspaper, hay residue, bone meal, lime and aged grass clippings to my raised bed soils. I introduce additional earthworms to my aged soil mix, augmenting those that will migrate to the beds on their own. The lowly earthworm has been called the earth's plowman. It's has the habit of burrowing down deep into the subsoils mixing everything in it's gullet, enriching it as it passes through and providing good drainage at the same time.

Having built such a rich mix in which to grow plants, as well as encouraging the growth of millions of micro-organism, fungi and bacteria, and millions of earthworms, which benefits you and your soil mix, you certainly do not want to kill it. Two things normally used in gardens will kill the life found in soil we have painstakingly built. One is insecticides used to control invaders to our plants. Insecticides will not discriminate between good bugs and bad bugs, it kills them all. It also will poison the soil, killing bacteria and earthworms that are doing a good job for us. The second item normally used in our gardens is commercial fertilizers. These add nutrients which will help the plants while it kills the same bacteria and earthworms we have encouraged. This is due to the residual salts left from using them. If you just have to use either, use natural insecticides or retardants and natural occurring components of the nitrogen, potash or phosphoreus.

Chapter 7

THE END TIMES

Bible scholars of every age, of every denomination, either religious or secular cannot and will not agree upon even a simple definition of the meaning of the term: End-Times. The one and only thing I find upon which they can all agree is that the Holy Bible references a period of time associated with the return of Jesus the Christ. This period in question, did it begin when Jesus ascended into heaven after His death and resurrection, does the End-Times begin at the time of His return, or several years prior to His return. The scholars cannot agree, each have a theory, so for purposes of explanation of the seventeen happenings they do agree upon, I will assume the End-Times or countdown begins when Jesus ascended into heaven after His death and resurrection, about 2000 years ago.

To further complicate matters, these same scholars cannot agree upon which of the prophesied happenings precede the beginning of the End-Times, which occur within the frame work of the End-Times period and what event or events signify a completion point of the End-Times. Rather than attempt to outguess the scholars, who cannot agree, I will try to lay a foundation of understanding by using the fulfillment of certain milestones, as prophesied. These most scholars do agree on.

There are seventeen milestones or events identified in the prophesies concerning these matters in the Holy Bible which the bible scholars do agree on in general. Each scholar may have a slightly different interpretation of this event and its implications and this is where the primary differences lie. I will list them in an accepted chronological order without any consideration that there may be some time overlaps. You will also note that one of the milestones is actually referenced as End-Times milestone. This really just references a series of accumulated events that will be observable throughout the world and is like a moment of time when things will begin to accelerate. I will leave the discussion and interpretation of all of these to those learned scholars. The milestones are:

1. Christ's promise to return for followers.
2. The Holy Spirit is Sent into the world as promised.
3. The Jews are scattered throughout the world as promised.
4. The Dome of The Rock is built upon the Temple Site.
5. The Jews Return Home to Israel.
6. The Jews gain Control of the Temple Area.
7. The Signs of the End-Times.
8. The Dome of The Rock is removed.
9. A period or time of World Distress.
10. The Rapture—Christians are taken up to heaven.
11. First Half of the Period of Tribulations.
12. Last Half of the Period of Tribulations.
13. The Beginning of Armageddon.
14. Christ and the Holy Ones return from Heaven.
15. Tribulation period Ends.
16. The Judgment of the Gentiles.
17. The Millennium.

I make no proclamations nor any defense as to the accuracy or order of these milestones. I only present them in the order generally accepted and generally labeled by most Bible scholars.

Many minor acts of various peoples throughout the world are needed to bring about any one of these major identified milestones. Take number one for instance. Before Jesus could make this promise, He had to first be tried by the government, convicted, put to death, buried and arise from the dead. In this process, He became the first risen, the Christ promised long ago and now could promise that He would return for us, His followers. Since this is true concerning each and every one of the seventeen milestones, its completion is not so easily pinpointed to an exact period of time. There are so many subtle parts going on, all over the world that are serving as building stones, if you will, for the completion of just one milestone and this may have profound influences upon other " in progress" happenings.

Awareness of these building stones identified in the light of these minor and subtle happenings aid us in certain deductions. We can say, as related to a major milestone for instance, this must occur before this major milestone can possibly occur. To illustrate, the Jews cannot control the Temple Area without first returning home. Now the reality is, for we can look back in history, the Jews returned home in 1948 and gained control of the Temple Area in 1967. One thing had to occur logically before the second could. I think we are experiencing now three of these minor and subtle happenings which must occur and serve as building blocks for the completion of one or more of the remaining milestones.

The three minor and subtle happenings that I think are occurring or are on the verge of occurring are as follows:

1. The fall of the United States as a world leader;

2. The reestablishment of Russia, in some form of the old USSR, as a world power in a communistic facade, non-democratic entity; and

3. The continued festering, tumultuous, revengeful,   terroristic uniting of the Arab nations.

These serve only as yardsticks of things to come, symptoms of circumstances taking place in the world which will trigger the setting of the stage for the completion of other major milestones.

The three events are not listed in order of time, nor have I attempted to identify which major milestone is dependent upon which of these occurrences.

I am not a prophet in any form of the imagination so the following scenarios and peoples involved serve only as suggestions of possibilities that could and probably will occur. The personalities and dates only serve to aid you in understanding how one event triggers another event. If you are a supporter of President Clinton, I apologize. I have used him as one personality because his recent actions are the most current and best to depict the potential danger such conduct can have, which results in the discontinuance of unity of the people of our nation. All timed events are speculations on my part, but hold strong possibilities of becoming reality within the lifetime of this generation.

Chapter 8

HIDEAWAY CAVE

I continued to explore the property and enjoy the view and I was experiencing, luckily, a superb harvest of fresh vegetables. The soil in the raised beds was aging very nicely and my compost piles were providing additive material for dressing the bed tops. Life was great and you just can't beat the taste of a meal comprised of foods you grow, harvest and prepare your self.

While exploring one day, near the cave I had turned into a root cellar, I came upon another cave. Now this didn't surprise me so much, knowing the history of these second oldest mountains of these United States. These mountains, not really mountains, are five hundred million years old. They are what is left of what use to be high plateaus. Over the eons of time, erosion from ice, sand, wind and water fashioned them into what we see today. The whole of the Ozarks have numerous caves left after the waters dissolved the limestone understructure of the high plateaus.

So, the cave I found this time was almost twice the size of the root cellar cave. At its depth was a trickle of water which emerged from the cave wall and then almost as quickly disappeared, after running above ground about five feet, under the facing wall. I wondered if this was the water source for my outside spring? One day I would try to find out. There is a very easy means of doing this with dyes.

You put the dye in the upstream part of the flow and check for its presence downstream. I didn't know if the underground portion would possibly filter the dye out beyond recognition. Oh well, it would be interesting and fun to find out.

The circumstances being reported in the news lead me to be concerned enough to contemplate the need to have a secondary residence. Nothing fancy, more like a hunting or fishing camp I use to see as a young lad. These were always very rustic, and to me as a young boy, exciting. When I saw the cave, as large as it was, I thought it just might be the answer.

Whether a true cabin hideaway, or this cave modified to serve as a hideaway, there were certain prerequisites that it had to fulfill. It had to be situated such that it would almost be impossible to be found. The hideaway had to be naturally camouflaged. Someone looking for such a place or perhaps a hunter would not notice anything out of the ordinary if they passed near. If circumstances of the world economic crises continued the way I foresaw, I would not want to be found.

Another prerequisite is the hideaway had to be reasonably close to the root cellar cave and a source of water. Accommodations for cooking secretly and the elimination of waste would have to be available without great effort and exposure. There had to be multiple access paths to and from the hideaway. Frequent use of the same access path would ware on the trail, becoming obvious to its purpose. There were other things but these were the primary one's I considered at the time.

I studied the new cave, using these prerequisites as a yard stick. The interior of the cave could easily be walled in for comfort. Petroleum gas could be used as a cooking fuel and vented to the outside, thus eliminating observation of smoke and noxious gases accumulation. It's entry could be approached from three different paths and the opening could be better camouflaged. It was only five hundred feet from the root cellar, not too far for convenience and not too close for detection of both if one or the other was found.

The only remaining prerequisite was waste management. This was material left over from food products and human. This could be easily solved if I used a composting approach. Now, there was no way I would ever use this composted material on the garden but composting eliminated odor and flies. I began looking for a depression beside the various trails away from the direction of the root cellar and hideaway caves. I finally found what I was looking for. It was a place I could get to quite easily, far enough off the path for concealment and deep enough to hold enough material to compost.

So with these major problems solved, I walled in the inside of the cave, put a rough flooring in, built shelves, set up my cooking area and constructed built-in bunks. The cooking fumes were vented, via pipe, to the outside and concealed from view. Most cooking would need to be done at night anyway. I had two rooms, one for sleeping and the other for sitting, cooking and eating. I only hoped the use of this space would not arise and if it did, it would only be of short duration.

Even so, I would be better off than most people who had not foreseen the potential of world crisis. It was rather sad, the thought of our world changing so rapidly and people going crazy from despair and hunger. The stress out there must be tremendous.

Being alone, being in danger of detection and being shut off from the outside world will gradually tell on the mind of the strongest. I had never been tested in such a way, and did not know the quality of my resolve or endurance. One thing I did know was I did not like to remain idle. If I could not have music, the television, only an occasional radio program, then I would need to provide my own outlets of expression of interest.

I stocked shelves of books, some of which I had read and others not. They were classics, poetry, how-to, technical as related to the earth and plants and general homesteading books. I just might need to know how to go back to earlier technology. I also included books on herbs and foraging. The worst would be if I actually had to use these.

In addition to books, I stocked up on painting materials. Though I am not a trained painter, I have enjoyed at times trying and find it a very interesting way of passing the time. I also stocked up on writing material so I might make notes on events, or write short stories or more poems. I really did not want to keep a journal as some would but I did want the ability to note interesting events.

So now I was reasonably ready for the worst, short of atomic warfare. I could survive, with luck, perhaps one year without adding anything in the way of food and basic necessities. With more luck, I might be able to replenish some of the perishables, from season to season.

Chapter 9

COMPOSTING

Under the circumstances being portrayed in this book, you would not think that I would suggest going to the trouble of composting organic materials. As the theme unfolds, the reason will be made clear and it is better to be prepare for both the worst and the best of times.

Composting is the process of altering a natural event to meet our needs in a more timely fashion. Organic materials decompose at the pace that nature designed but composting uses this decomposition by nature, improves on the design by putting the various elements of this process into a more managed and useful manner.

When leaves, for instance, fall upon the earth, they are immediately attacked by bacteria, fungi and possibly earthworms and other creepy crawly things. The end product is "decomposed leaf material" called leaf mold. Eventually, it will become humus and be incorporated in the "topsoil" around the tree base. The leaves can not add anything to the topsoil that was not originally there before but is still useful as an additive to the soil.

Composting is the process of incorporating various materials of an organic origin into a homogeneous mix, in which air and water flow can be controlled, maximizing the decomposition of the whole. Now, to me, that is so much jargon to confuse the average person and does not convey anything of use. This is how

I want to compost, I gather leaves, grass clippings, small twigs, any manure I can find, vegetable trimmings and maybe some garden soil. I place a layer of this, and a layer of that, until I have used all of the materials I have gathered. If it were a sandwich, it would look kind of like a Dagwood sandwich, you know the cartoon character, but without the bread.

All I am trying to do, is to maximize the decomposition process, create an environment which encourages the multiplying of the aerobic bacteria and fungi. There will be multiple other micro organisms in this moist mixture and their combined efforts will decompose the organic material very quickly. If I do not let it get too wet, I will only have aerobic bacteria. Too wet, and I will get anaerobic bacteria, the kind in sewer ditches and with them I will get a very offensive odor.

Let me illustrate my method and by far the easiest composting structure I have ever used. First, I construct a round cage using welded wire. This wire you can get from any hardware store, and your hardwareman will know what I am talking about. The gage of the wire is not important and the spaces just a little more so. I like the one inch by one inch but that is because it happen to be what I had at the time I constructed my first cage. I also like the width of the wire to be four foot, because this is a good working height once you make your cage. The pen is just a length of this welded wire laid out and the two cut ends pulled back together so they overlap about four inches. I use baling wire or you can use the wire from a coat hanger to tie the two cut ends together. Now you have a cage with an open top and bottom, and it should be about four or five foot in diameter.

I like to build at least two of these cages, of course leaving the top and bottom open. Place the cages under a nice shade tree that will allow about a foot or two between the cages and space enough for two more cages of the same size. Now I have two cages with the bottoms on the ground, waiting for organic material. The first layer into the cage can be anything you have accumulated, but I prefer using oak leaves. Oak leaves have a tendency to pack and it is this packing which I want to take advantage. This aids in excluding root growth from the bottom up from the tree, and aids in the retention of moisture. You can start with anything, plastic, newspaper, or anything organic, non fatty.

The layers are all about six inches, and please use your eye to measure, it is not that critical. Start with something like the oak leaves, followed by grass clipping, cow manure, other leaves, straw, garden soil, hay, other manures, vegetable trimmings, more soil, newspaper, leaf mold if you have it, small twigs, sawdust, manures, soil, grass clippings and so on and so on. The order or relationship of one material to another is not so very important until you get experience. Once you have experience, you will learn what material best go with another in order for the whole process to be accelerated. The main thing now is to understand, you can use any organic material in conjunction with any other organic material. There are two exceptions that I caution you about. Never put your tomato or Irish potato stems/stalks in the compost pile, they belong to the night shade family and are poisonous. The second item is the fats from animals. These will encourage vermin which you do not want.

A very good rule of thumb about layering is to mix the texture of the various materials. A coarse texture followed by a fine textured material is better than say small twigs followed by coarse straw. I would suggest you do it this way. Small twigs followed by grass clippings and then the coarse straw perhaps followed by cow manure. You need not be concerned so much after the first layering process but when you can, this is a good practice. Again, when you first start a pile, you are not likely to fill your first cage. So, create a depression in the center to direct the rain water or your hose water toward the center of the pile. Do this each time you add material until the cage is full.

The two important factors other than the organic material is for the material to be aerated and kept moist. Alternating texture of the organic material and the spacing in the wire cages provide aeration with ease. You do not have to be concerned with this requirement as long as you have followed my guide lines. Moisture is almost as easy. If the weather is on the dry side, just spray the pile with your garden hose until you think the water has percolated throughout the pile. When in doubt, just push your hand down into the mix and you will be able to tell if you need more water. Otherwise, do not over water, let nature takes its course. One thing you will notice, when you put your arm down into the pile is the heat. That means the pile is working, and the bacteria are doing their job.

When one cage is full, start on the second cage. It takes about four weeks for a cage of material to age to the point it needs turning. Use the four week period as a rule of thumb. The composition of organic material you use will vary from time to time and the speed in which you fill one cage and need to use your second is hard to determine ahead of time. What I normally do is when one cage is full, I start filling the second. I remove the first cage from around the pile and place the emptied cage near the uncaged pile. The material of the uncaged pile is still on the course side, especially on the outside area. So, I use a pitchfork to transfer the old pile material into the cage it came from. I prefer to have the outside material of the pile placed near the center of the turned pile. This is a form of mixing while turning my aged pile into the cage, forming a new composition. As I am transferring this old material, I may notice that it may need additional moisture so I add water in a spray during the turning process. The last little bit of the pile, which was oak leaves in my pile, may have to be moved by using a shovel.

So each time a cage is filled, and a new cage is begun, I turn the old material by removing the cage, placing the cage near and transfer the pile without the cage into its former cage. The pitchfork gives me leverage to do the work easily, and the aged material is lighter than before from having partially decomposed, so no back pains. You will note that the pile has shrunk during the aging process. This is normal. During the next turning you will also find that most of the material can be used for top dressing the soils in your raised bed or even as a potting soil. Use any amount of this older pile as you need. The remaining amount can be incorporated with the material in your second cage or left in its present cage and new material added right on top of it.

If you now understand the very basics of composting, you will be able to repeat the process in a less than ideal environment. While roaming over my acreage close to the root cellar cave and over toward the hideaway cave, I am always searching for natural depressions in the terrain. What I look for are places that received enough sunlight that could be used for alternative garden spots. Using the composting method, I could gradually add organic materials to the material already there, especially manures. In this way, I could let nature take its course until such time as I just might need these spots.

My thinking was this. Should the day come that I needed to move to the hideaway cave, I probably would not be able to use my raised beds for food production. I knew from experience that the native soils around my farm were too poor to produce good healthy plants. If I could prepare these possible spots in advance, I would at least be able to plant the winter type vegetables. These would blend better into a natural look than most of the warmer weather plants. Scattered as they would naturally be, their detection would be more difficult and most people would just think I was using them to attract game. I have tried to think of the worst possible series of events and prepare contingency plans to over-come the adversity of these situations.

A last note about composting. Composting can be a lot of hard work, or minimized as I have tried to do. In 1934 and again in 1964, the United States Department of Agriculture declared our farm lands were depleted of minerals. This means that our source of minerals for our own bodies cannot and will not come from plants grown in these soils. I personally believe this is a primary reason we are seeing almost an epidemic increase in certain diseases.

You will note that I have included in my organic material list such items as tree leaves, and sawdust and small twigs. The root systems of trees grow deep, in mineral rich soils. These minerals are taken up by the trees and stored in various chemical complexes in parts of the tree body and leaves. By adding them to my compost material, I am adding needed minerals back to my diet when I eat the foods grown in the resulting soil. I had not mentioned the use of lime, whether natural or agriculture lime, but even crushed limestone could be sprinkled in your compost pile mix. One other source of lime I have used is crushed wallboard. The chalky substance between the outer paper layers is about a sixty five percent calcium based material. Micro-organisms can do wonders with this material. Pulverized bone, crab and lobster shells and even egg shells contain calcium. Use your imagination and you will find a source in your area for almost anything mineral or organic. Old coffee beans over cooked, or food processing plant waste, for instance. Look and you will find.

Chapter 10

A DIVIDED NATION

It is predicted that the United States will not be a factor in the chain of events that must occur prior to the return of the Christian Christ. Some will agree and others will not. Here are the symptoms or preliminary events that are leading us toward the downfall of the United States, as I see them.

In 1991, with almost world wide coalition against Iraq, including the majority of Arab nations, we had the best and only chance of destroying Iraq. Iraq is not the place but will serve as the final trigger for the on coming of the Biblical Armageddon. So in reality, it could not be destroyed in 1991 during Dessert Storm. Even so, Dessert Storm was the one and only chance the world had or will have for destroying Iraq until the actual Armageddon.

Then in late 1997, President Clinton began setting the stage for another symptom that would lead to the downfall of our nation, as we know it. By the beginning of 1999, the point of no return had already been reached. It would make no difference whether he was removed from office or not. Our nation had already embraced a position that would not allow the continuance of the United States role as a world leader. Through his own personal guilt of immoral sex, abuse of power, lying while under oath, and obstruction of justice, Mr. Clinton set the stage for a divided nation. It no longer mattered whether his accusers or his defenders were right. The accusers became the self-righteous Republicans, so-called by many of the Democrats, with a perceived vendetta against Mr. Clinton. The Democrats became the self proclaimed defenders of what was holy (the presidency) of a nation, the voice of the people. The truth of the matter is that both sides played politics at what ever the cost. Our people are divided as they have never been and a divided nation will not stand.

Of all the other symptoms of a nation falling, the most obvious is the one caused again by President Clinton. Whether he caused the attack upon Iraq during Dessert Fox for his own personal agenda or not will have to be judged by others. The fact that the spoken objectives were not met in truth puts a great shadow upon the timing of the approved attack. The resulting estrangement of our nation with almost all the Arab world was crucial in our efforts to remain among the world leaders in influencing the conscience of the nations of the world. Mr. Clinton's private personal conduct through his own continued denial was world news and became a focal point of embarrassment of all the world to see and experience.

The resulting Impeachment, put further strain upon the peoples of our nation Strong feelings emerged with party against party as had never before existed. Sure, the two parties have always had their differences, their own agenda, but never had any event of the past created such a festering sore of un-forgiveness and attitude of impending revenge. Threats from the Democrat circles threatening those of the Republican circle with statements like "You will pay for this vote of impeachment". It was like a call to arms or a rallying cry. And all the time, the world watched and wondered seriously about a nation's people who could follow such a man.

President Clinton gave them their answer. We were a nation drawing lines in the sand. Daring the other side to cross over, playing politics with strong partisan agendas, while the unity of the nation fell apart. Mr. Clinton's authorization of an attack upon Iraq served only to unit the Arab world and other major players against the self appointed role of the United States as the policeman of the world. This act more than any other he might have made forged his name upon history, not as he had hoped. Rather than Mr. Clinton's legacy being among world leaders who had the influence to better the world, Mr. Clinton will be most remembered for his failure to understand the Arab mind set. For perpetrating events that would unit the Arab world. An Arab world in which would develop a fanatical hatred for a nation of infidels, we of the United States. Mr. Clinton just served as an instrument of prophecy, his actions the catalyst, for someone had to be the modern day Judas.

The downfall of a nation, any nation, can never be attributed to one man. So it is in our imminent downfall. Mr. Clinton's personal conduct would not have been tolerated, just a few years back. The nation, not just one party, would have been appalled by such behavior and immediate removal action would have been demanded by the majority. This toleration of such blatant behavior is merely an indication of the acute breakdown of the moral fiber of a people. History truly repeats itself, far every great fallen nation has followed the same path, acceptance of promiscuity on a grand scale. We all develop our individual value systems, but when we allow others to flaunt theirs with impunity, our own is weakened in the process. The poet said that "no man is an island". What one person or groups of people perform morally, either good or evil, affects all. So when our nation falls, and it surely will, we the people must be considered to be at the heart of the cause and effect. We the people let it happen. Our forefathers founded this nation, seeking God, or religious freedom. When did we accept a less honorable goal?

Chapter 11

LIVING ABUNDANTLY

One of the fascinating prospects I encountered when I realized that I was really going to move to the NW corner of Arkansas was I would be able to put all the pieces of my life's dream together. Can you just imagine fifty years of believing that a man could obtain a very small piece of land, put the various self-sustaining ideas in place and see it really happen, just as he had dreamed.

None of the various projects I have written about have I not done. I have had a root cellar, for instance, but it wasn't in a cave that was modified to accommodate this function. I have lived off the land for upward of two weeks in the swamps of Louisiana with nothing more than a knife, a tarp, a bag of salt and some hooks, line and sinkers, oh, and one cast iron skillet. I forced myself to learn what could be eaten and what to avoid. What a great time.

I want to give you a short list of other possible projects that a person might consider important in his scheme of things, for his survival. There is no way I can provide all the technical information one would need to make these things happen. The library is a great source of information and so is the Internet. If a person really wants answers, they are out there. Should that same person find any item useful, then I recommend adding a book on the subject to their library. We all need reference books in areas of our interest and pursuit. In this chapter I want to introduce you to a most ancient agriculture practice, hydroponics.

Early in the 50's, while still in college, I got into a conversation with one of my science professors and was asking perhaps some very naive questions. During this conversation, with the professor being so gracious not to make me appear completely stupid, he responded to some question I had asked by asking me a question. He ask me had I "ever heard of hydroponics?". Of course, my answer was in the negative. Since it seemed to him that this was more or less in keeping with the answer I was pursuing, he suggested I look up the word and do some research on the subject. Isn't that just like a professor, he had the answer but wanted me to do the work on my own rather than just sharing his knowledge. He really did me a great service that day.

Hydroponics is basically the growing of various plants in a soil-less environment using the necessary nutrients needed by the plant, dissolved and carried by water to the root system. In my research, I found that hydroponics were as ancient as the Gardens of Babylon. Some form of it had been practiced in China for over 4000 years. In modern hydroponics practices, pre-prepared chemicals are dissolved in water, this water is allowed to flow through channels over which plants are suspended with but their roots dangling into the channels. The liquid is received in a tank at the end of the down flow and returned to the original tank at the beginning. One of the dangers of hydroponics of this type is the accumulation of salts, the requirement of constantly having to monitor the chemical mix and the expense of the pre-prepared chemicals.

Let us suppose that we are sitting on the bank of a stream with our feet dangling in the water. Our feet then are like the root system of a plant which can absorb the nutrients in the water. Our bodies are on the bank, or like the stems or trunks of the plants suspended from Styrofoam or some other suitable material. Now in the water are dissolved nutrients which come from rainwater running through leaf mold under the trees, across gravel being eroded by the water flow and absorption of air components as it splashed across rocks in its way. So we merrily sit on the bank, absorb these nutrients through our little pinkies and we grow. That would be hydroponics as applied to we humans.

Since I didn't like the use of limited chemical mixes, I experimented with other sources of the necessary nutrients. I had access to an almost limitless supply of manures from dairy cows, horse stall rentals and chicken farmers. My cost was time, energy, hauling and determination. I took these fine products and placed them in a barrel and filled with water. I had put a drain at the bottom of the barrel so I could direct the flow of water were I desired. Some people have referred to this liquid as "Texas Tea", no offense, so I will refer to it as tea.

This tea liquid is not generally recycled as would be in commercial hydroponic liquids. Instead I let it flow through the channel, on out into a lagoon, lower than the hydroponic unit. Later the liquid would be used to water the outdoor garden or greenhouse plants. Anyway, I had this mixture of manure and water, and as the tea began to lose its color at the drain end I had to make new tea. The first batch of manure would be used, with water refills, from two to three times before a new batch had to be made.

What was left of the barrel contents was the insoluble portion of manure. This wet and soggy mess went into my compost pile, a layer of the mess, followed by some drier organic material and so on until I had it properly incorporated into the compost pile. The barrel was refilled with more or less dry manures, water added and I had a new batch of tea.

One thing that in the real practice of hydroponics that differs from my little story of dangling feet is in a stream, the liquid flows always and would leave our feet in the water at all times. In hydroponic practices, the roots are not submerged in the liquid, constantly. Stones are commonly used so the roots may anchor themselves and the stones will retain surface moisture which the roots will utilize. Sand is also occasionally used. The point is that roots of most plants are not adapted to withstand submersion for long periods of time and will rot if forced to endure such measures. So the tea is applied several times daily at set intervals of time.

Other structures may be used to utilize the practice of hydroponics. I have constructed a serpentine rack of PVC four inch pipe ending in a drain end over a five gallon bucket. At the drain end, I actually have to have several five gallon buckets, or the same number of those used to transport the tea in. The drain end is plugged with a wooden plug I build for that purpose so no tea drains out until I have the whole unit filled. In that way, all the roots are temporarily submerged in the fluid.

The beginning of the serpentine rack of pipes is an elbow, left open so it serves as a means to pour the tea. The vertical joints are just two elbows with a coupler and attaches to the next horizontal pipe. So your tea will flow from one horizontal pipe to the next until it finally empties into the drain bucket. Since none of the joints are permanently attached or cemented, I re-enforce them by stretching nylon cord from vertical joint to vertical joint. The fluid does not create great pressure, but then again, I don't want to have to mop it up.

Along the horizontal members, every four inches, I cut slots of two inches by two inches. I can use Styrofoam block of this size to plug any unused slot but also to support the plants to be grown in this pipe rack. If the rack is totally vertical, that is one horizontal pipe only twelve inches directly over another horizontal pipe, and so on, then you can only grow plants that do not get very tall. If you support the rack at an angle, and the slots are still on the upper most part of the horizontal pipe, you can grow larger plants, such as tomatoes. These units can be disassembled and cleaned or moved to other convenient areas.

Another method you can use is a series of hanging baskets, one suspended from the one above it and so on. The separation of one basket to the one above will also determine the size plant you may use. Once you have this arranged, just pour the tea in the top basket and the excess fluid will drip down into the second, it into the third. A bucket can be placed under the last basket should you need to. This method is messy but you take advantage of space by using them vertically.

Chapter 12

THE CRISIS BEGINS

In the Spring of 2000, I had planted my second crop in my raised bed garden. I certainly hoped this years harvest would be better than the first. I realized that the first year's failure was primarily due to the freshness of the soil mix and this would not be indicative of seceding planting and harvest. There seemed to be an urgency in my mind, in my soul this year that had been absent last Spring. The world news was depressing and things appeared not to be just right in spite of the assurance of our world leaders.

Brazil had a tremendous set back just when it looked like its economy was turning around. The best thing to be said about that is it curtailed the destruction of the rain forest. Several other large nations were on the brink of disaster but the world leaders were optimistic toward their recovery. All of this was to be expected due to the awareness of the major industrial nations' efforts toward Y2K compliance. Contingency plans had been well formed to assist those struggling to overcome this event's inconveniences. I wonder if Brazil was aware of these contingency plans.

How many small third world countries were failing? How much impact were their failures having on the world economy? Why was this information not being reported?

With these questions in my mind, it became obvious why I felt anxious and had a sense of urgency. I had to complete the root cellar, which would be my refuge, food wise. I had to continue to improve the orchard. Seems like I had always been trimming and grafting and planting. The benefits of the effort was beginning to be evident. I had found the year around spring and I needed to complete the retaining wall just in case I needed another source of water.

Time seemed so short.

Chapter 13

THE RUSSIANS

The second primer performer upon the world stage that had to change before taking its role in the affairs of Biblical prophecy was Russia. The downfall of communist USSR was heralded by the free world as the end of the cold war. The world rejoiced to see the collapse of the USSR and the re-emergence of independent sovereign nations free to chose their own destinies. Russia would become democratic, and take its proper role of leadership toward peace and prosperity. Little did the world realize this was only a temporary reprieve.

Russia and its leaders never made a complete commitment to a democratic form of government nor a capitalistic form of commerce. There continued to be the distractors, pouncing on every little set back, threatening the experimenters with being kicked out and being replaced with a true government, of the old order. It was proving to be too difficult to change their spots, the old ways may not have been perfect, but at least they were understood.

Russia tried this new economic order, held its hand out for support every time things didn't happen as fast as her peoples believed it should. We always were there to bail them out, totally justified since this was cheaper than the cold war had been. And besides, Russia is now our friend. They too, watched the events of 1998.

Russia during 1997 and 1998, added another player to the already failing economy. Their presidency was in jeopardy and the United States government's hands were tied. We just could not interfere with the political arena of Russia, yet we certainly did not want a new president who's leanings were communistic. We parried and thrust with a delicate touch lest we offend our new political friend.

Now, two preliminary events occurred that pushes Russia back to her old ways. The first has been discussed but bares some review. Our attack upon Iraq incensed the Russians against us. They were appalled at our audacity to project ourselves as policemen of world affairs. Our close political relationship was altered irreparably forever. There would certainly be overtones of reconciliation but the clock could not be turned back. The die had been cast for each of our nations to play our part on a much larger world stage.

The second nail being driven into Russia's coffin, its political future was just one year away. Y2K was to stick its ugly head up, disrupt the world's economy like nothing else and Russia would be one of the first major industrialized nations to fail. Even in 1998, Russia was in such financial straits, that it was hard to believe that it could survive 1999. Had the United States picked up its marbles and gone home because Russia didn't support her against Iraq, Russia would have most likely failed in 1999.

The year 2000 brought its own type of panic. Third world countries economies were failing right and left. Many of these were such small players in world economy that little domino effects were being felt. As always in the domino effect, once the action starts, who can really tell where it ends. This small country failed, no one notices, but it effects a neighbor. That neighbor failed, effecting yet another country just a little further up on the development ladder.

This was the world stage of the early part of year 2000. The world economy still looked promising. Sure there were some set backs but all this had been predicted. As the year 2001 approached a few larger countries failed, then Brazil. Things begin to really pick up when major banks of Japan were either taken over by the government or just allowed to completely fail. No one seem to know what actions to take, so none was being taken.

Early 2001, Russia experiences a financial collapse. It had lost its ability to compete on the world market front. Russia's only major export continued to be military equipment. Iran and Syria continued to purchase tools of war from Russia under the unbelieving watchful eyes of their neighbors and Israel. Even so, the internal political chaos was such that there were no more options to exercise. Their world trade nations could not buy, they could not sell. Democracy had failed, capitalism had failed, at least in Russia.

Now Russia's fate, its future was predestined. Only the passage of time was required before Russia would re-emerge upon the world stage in a most shocking manner. They would rebuild their armies, their national pride. They would become an enormous hibernating bear of a country, caught in a long, fitful winter sleep. Just when everyone else was seemingly distracted by other world events, the sleeping bear would awaken. When it looked out of its den, what it would see was an opportunity to gain some control by supplying its best customers with arms and military know how. Little did she (Russia) realize that she would be dragged (hooked in the jaw) into the war of wars by her Arab allies, and that her armies would be all but destroyed. The war to control the whole of Asia Minor was set, while destroying the Arabs' avowed enemy, Israel.

Sympathy toward Russia might be appropriate, her peoples prayed for, this potentially great nation who had given us greatness in music and ballet, was doomed when she was founded. She had never accepted a course directed toward God but one seeking the ultimate power of man. Her financial fall was a great humiliation, in her financial recovery she must then be magnanimous. Only one item, one marketable object remained in her possession, one profitable export she could sell, this her ability to compete on the world market in the development and reproduction of arms. This achievement still reminded the world of her past greatness, so turning her back on all opposition she sold arms to anyone who could purchase them, either with oil or cash.

When men get desperate, they become irrational and do foolish things, like selling arms to a people who had gone mad with hatred for any who did not believe their way, but especially full of hatred toward Israel.

Chapter 14

WORST OF TIMES

World news of country after country failing, layoffs sweeping the nation as company after company had to have "cutbacks", and even cities of our own rich nation finding it difficult to remain solvent, I found this all to be terribly disheartening. I seemed to be caught up in a world becoming unsettled and I felt helpless. Today, as at other times, I tried to picture in my mind how it would be if this became the worst of times.

I remembered my youth, a time when we still had an outhouse, you know the kind with a half moon cut in the door panel. I remember using the kerosene lamps, the ball jars filled with canned fruits, peas and other vegetables. My grandfather's smoke house, with its wonderful aroma , full of hams, bacon slabs and sausages. He always had what seemed to me more food either canned or smoked than he and my grandmother would ever need. Even when the families would gather for special events, most brought their favorite dishes and all would be placed on tables out under the trees, like a church social.

To walk into my grandmother's kitchen, during these times, when she and my mother and my aunts were preparing for this wonderful meal at our family gathering was just a delight. The smell of fresh bread or biscuits baking just made my mouth water, I could hardly wait to slap some butter, real butter, on a slice of fresh bread or a hot biscuit and oh, what a taste. We city people have forgotten what fresh churned, salty butter taste like. These were very special times in my youth.

I remembered our entertainment of the time, a radio. At night, we as a family, would sit around listening to "The Great Geldersleeve", or "Amos and Andy", or "Fibber McGee and Molly". Who could forget programs like "The Shadow" or "The Grand Ole Oprey". I remember that nearly every Sunday morning of my youth, my mother would tune the radio to KWKH of Shreveport, Louisiana. Then on the airwaves we would always hear "Turn your radio on, and listen to the music of the air, get in touch with God, turn your radio on". Those of that generation will remember the tune. It still gives me pleasure when I remember.

Now, the foods people have, someone else pre-prepared it for us. Many people have forgotten the art of providing for themselves. If it can't be purchased, they do without. Even those of us who still grow vegetables in a garden have minimized the labor of preserving these wonderful foods by using a freezer. Few of us preserve foods in glass jars, even fewer remember how. What happens to us if we no longer have electricity, or the small farmer who will sell us his fresh vegetables, or stores cannot keep their shelves stocked and we have not stocked up for bad times. It is a frightening thought.

I looked out at all the vegetables growing in my raised beds and the bountiful harvest that I would have from my restored orchard of fruit trees. One of the greatest pleasure I have experienced in life is when I produced more than I could possibly use, I gave to families who needed. It did not matter to me that they never knew that I was the one who left it on their doorsteps. I just wanted to share. Under the impending circumstances, perhaps I could still perform this kindness, but I also was conscious that I had to learn how to preserve this bounty, just in case things did continue to worsen.

I had canned foods over the years using a pressure cooker, a steaming pot and those wonderful ball jars. I new how to make jellies and preserves out of fruits, to pickle cucumbers and eggs and had tried pickling okra. Over the years I had collected books on the subject and had the equipment but the books had long been stored away and the equipment had been given away. I needed to acquire new equipment and fresh supplies of various sized jars and lids. Just like most people, I now froze foods for later use, for now I had electricity.

At one time, years ago, I had gotten interested in dehydrating foods. There were so many devices that companies wanted to sell that claimed to be the ultimate in dehydration of vegetables and fruits. All of them required power, electrical power. I had tried building my own, but found the best method, well maybe not the best method, but at least the least expensive method was a cone shaped hood in which trays could be placed.

The hood sat about six inches off a concrete floor, and was in full sunlight. I painted it black in order to absorb more heat. It had an access door that allowed me to place or remove the trays of sliced vegetables or fruits. Each tray, which had a wire bottom, had its own shape and assigned place within the hooded chamber. The idea was for the hooded chamber to heat up, causing an upward air flow. This convected air would draw fresh outside air through the bottom of the hood passing through the various foods and out the top which was a six inch chimney pipe.

This device worked so well and I could dehydrate so much food, I built two more, all placed in the full sun. I stole one idea from the roofing industry and placed a revolving cap on the chimney pipe. This prevented rain from entering the chamber and served as an extra drawing of air by the vacuum created by wind being blown across this device. Dehydrated foods will keep and look better if stored away from sunlight and in a cool place. So I would use ziplock freezer bags to store the foods. Each bag was labeled and placed in baskets which were then place on shelves in the root cellar.

One thing I did not use the dehydrator for was the dehydration of herbs. At first I had tried this but found that I lost so much of the tender leaf parts during the transferring of the dried product. The other reason I quite this practice is they seemed to take up too much of the room which could be better utilized by more important food items. I solved my problem by just laying the herbs on the concrete floor, in the full sun. Of course, these would have to be turned occasionally but the end product was worth the extra care. Once dried in this way, I would shred the leaves by placing a branch or stalk between my hands and rubbing them back and forth. This removed the delicate leaves and left most of the stem intact. After a little picking of the small stems that happened in the droppings, I would place the dried leafy material in small ziplock bags, label them and place these in the root cellar. There is no greater pleasure, to a cook, than to open up one of these selected bags and smell the marvelous aroma coming from the herb.

I did build a smokehouse and learned how to successfully preserve various meats. In good times, after having experienced this renewed pleasure, I promised myself to always have a smokehouse. When I put this practice back in the context of the current world decline, I realized that this method of preserving foods could not be relied upon. When things really got bad, the last thing you would want to do is draw attention to your presence in a given area. To cure meats in a smokehouse, as the name implies, you need smoke. Smoke can be seen from miles around. So this practice was stopped almost as fast as it had begun.

There were two methods of preserving meat I considered and later rejected. One was to preserve the meat by the salted meat method. Storing prepared meat encompassed in fats, was the other. I rejected both method more because of the thought of it, than for the shortcomings of the method. However, I did use the Indian's old standby which was to jerk some meats. This preserves meats very nicely, and like the dehydrated fruits, vegetables, and herbs, it can be stored in bags and placed in the root cellar.

I am of the opinion, that anyone can learn these simple methods and with care, store a goodly supply of foods away for future personal use or for gifts to others. There are a lot of foods, such as nuts and field dried legumes (peas and beans) that can be stored in their shell or placed in vermin proof containers for future consumption. These items along with native plants that can be foraged from the country side, can feed a family very well, indeed.

Chapter 15

THE OTHERS

Many people, when first considering the prospects of living the free life on a self-sustaining farm have all these grandiose ideas of having a cow, a tractor, a small cottage, and time to contemplate the mysteries of life. Perhaps, they will have a greenhouse and chickens and be able to raise a fatten calf and in some way, they will produce enough of something as a means for obtaining the gasoline and oil for their tractor, the few items they cannot produce, like salt and flour, or vinegar, medicines, clothes or sundry other necessities. All these things will just happen. They won't.

A farm is hard work and a luxury like a tractor is expensive. My approach has always been to put things in perspective, know what is important and what is not, identify ways to lessen the work load and at the same time produce as much as possible for the labor expended. For instance, I eliminated the need for a tractor by using raised beds for vegetables. I eliminated the need for fertilizers by composting and the need for insecticides by using natural solutions. I certainly could not afford a milk cow which would produce far too much milk than I could possibly drink or process into cheeses.

When I designed my barn and associated pens, walk ways and work areas, I wanted the work to progress from one task area toward the next most logical task area. To illustrate just a portion of this idea, the chicken coop backed up to the work area of the barn. The area of the chicken coop where the roost area was placed formed the back side of the coop adjacent to this work area. By raising a door that swung up and out of the way, from the work area space, I could rack the chicken manure onto the floor space, then close the door. This manure would be placed into a wheel barrow and I would then move down the line.

The adjoining space was where I milked and feed the milk goat. I would clean up this pen, place this material into the wheel barrow and moved to the next area. This next area was where I had my rabbit hutches. The same process was repeated until ultimately I arrived at the tank where I created my tea for use in my adjoining hydroponic unit. I think you have the idea. Work flowed from point to point in a logical order eliminating backtracking from here to yon. The feeding process followed the same path, from point to point until all the different stock was feed.

The major point I am trying to convey is running even a small farm can be a lot of hard work, but with a little thinking and planning, so much of the labor can be eliminated or at least lightened. Look for alternative ways of accomplishing your goal.

When a young man, I got interested in raising pigeons. I went out and bought several pair of the meat type pigeons and put them into a pen area that gave them room to fly some and had nest boxes. It wasn't long before they were nesting and soon to follow the hatching of the eggs. In just twenty eight days from hatching, the squabs were ready to be eaten or allowed to grow into maturity and join the ranks of breeders.

I found that should I let the purchased pigeons out to fly free, they may or may not come back to the pen. It didn't matter whether they were proud parents or not. More often than not, I lost those. So I quit doing that, but tried the young pigeons which had been reared in the pigeon pen. When they first put on their feathers and started trying to fly is the best time, I found, to try this experiment. Oh! They would take off and I would say to myself that I had made another mistake. But soon after they had a chance to test their wings, in they would soar and land atop the pen. I would put them back in the pen area and the first thing they wanted was food and water.

I thought to myself, if these young pigeons could be taught to do this consistently, it would prove to be a very good way to save money. I sat up another flight pen and nesting area just for the younger pigeons, those that would be allowed to fly freely. I monitored the feed consumption of these birds against those that were not allowed to fly freely. The flyers ate almost nothing, they were foraging for themselves and saving me a lot of money and labor. I decided from this experience to include pigeons in my plans for a self-sustaining farm.

As a kid, my family always had chickens which provided fresh eggs and of course Sunday dinner. I have very vivid memories of feeding the chickens chops, gathering eggs and when I finally got large enough being given the chore of ringing the chicken's neck, and plucking the feathers after dipping the dead bird in very hot water. It was so funny to me, not the chicken, to watch the chicken run around with out a head.

So it was natural for me to include chickens in my live stock list. I had long ago lost a taste for the mass produced chickens from the grocery store and wanted that taste I remembered from my youth. Another benefit from raising penned chickens is the free manure, which is very high in nitrogen. With little effort, the meat type chickens I purchased could be made broody, and in a very short time I would have baby chicks. One of the things I learned over the years is those hens that were allowed to forage had deeper colored egg yolks. Not that it was more nourishing but at least it was more attractive than the pale yellow of caged chickens.

This thought gave me an idea to try once I was actually on my little farm. Could I save money by allowing the chickens to forage for themselves during the day. This just might prove out to be almost as effective as the experiment conducted on the pigeons. One thing I did know, it could not hurt even if I lost a bird or two in time. One other thing I knew was I would still have to pen the chickens up at night to protect them against predators and to continue my source of their rich manure. By the way, feathers are a very good item to include in a compost pile, slow to break down but rich in nitrogen.

Many times during my youth, I remember the beautiful call of the guinea fowls my grandfather raised. You could not get within a half mile of my grandfather's farm without these birds, of African origin, setting off their alarming calls. They were better than any watch dog you could possibly have. These birds offered much to be desired in a farm of my type. Their meat was almost as good a chicken, their eggs were very good, they would forage for themselves, they never need penning and as already mentioned, they were excellent watch dogs, (birds).

One major fault they possessed was their habit of hiding their nest. If you wanted fresh eggs, daily, you had to look for their well hidden nest. Sometimes you would find it a little too late and boy, what a mess if you should break a spoiled egg. But all in all, they would merit a place on a self sustaining farm.

Milk is found in almost everyone's diet, either liquid or in some other dairy food product. It was hard for me at the beginning to consider not having a cow on my farm. When considered against the back drop of labor involved in obtaining the milk, processing and storing the milk, cost of feeding and the space to maintain the cow, I begin to look for a better solution. My solution came in the form of a milk goat, actually several.

A goat has many advantages for a small farm over a cow. If a goat is to be pastured, they require less space than a cow. Goats will forage for themselves, and eat almost any type plant. Their volume of milk is more in keeping with my daily needs, and can be processed into some wonderful cheeses. Cheeses can be stored for later use long after the goat quit producing milk.

Using battery powered electric fence units, I will be able to set off a sparsely wooded area near a water source for a goat foraging area. The native plants of low growing shrubs, trees, grasses and bramble will supply several goats with all the food they need. I plan to place a mineral-salt block next to a shed like structure. This structure will be where I give the goat some feed while I milk them. Since I have never done this, I may find that I must supplement their feed. In goats, I gain good easily digestible milk, a good product for cheese processing, a most tasty meat source and an animal that requires minimal feed cost, and labor.

Almost no meat more closely equates with the diversity of chicken meat than does the domestic rabbit. I know of no dish that you would normally use chicken that you could not use rabbit. These furry animals are easy to raise, a joy to watch and handle and are so low cost in maintaining, it is almost criminal. Feeding can come directly from nature if you are willing to do the foraging for them. They will eat almost any greenery. One thing to watch for, when a rabbit has been on pellet foods and then shifted direct to fresh greens, they get diarrhea badly. If you have to start your rabbits off on dry pellets, introduce the fresh greens gradually, weaning them away from the dry pellets slowly. Another thing to watch for is old or soiled greens. Feed the rabbits fresh greens, all they can eat in about fifteen minute, remove the remainder. Keep fresh and clean water before them at all times.

A very good way to maximize space on a small farm is to let the same area serve two or more purpose. Whether you use hanging cages or hutches for rabbits, the space below can be beneficially used to raise a very good friend to the farmer, the earthworm. I box in the underside of the cages, which will catch the dropping from the rabbits. Earthworms, or your garden, can use these droppings directly, without aging. I like to fill the box with a beginning of compost, place my starter worms within this and let nature, rabbits in this case, take its course. The worms will multiply like crazy and convert the rabbit manure and the compost material into a very rich soil additive for the raised bed soils. The earthworms themselves make a wonderful bait for fishing or when dried, a wonderful supplement to your pigeon and chicken feed.

In my original plans for a self-sustaining mini farm, I had planned for a greenhouse and possibly an electrical system powered by water. The world situation being what it is, has caused me to postpone the inclusion of these items. A greenhouse has many advantages for propagating plants, starting plants and growing off seasoned plants. Their greatest advantage is also their greatest disadvantage in troubled times, their required climate controlled environment. Unlike hydroponics, the technology used in a greenhouse cannot be easily used any where else but a greenhouse.

Considering an electrical service using a water driven power source, while perhaps practical on a small farm, is not practical on my small farm. I do not have the water source to drive the generator and even if I did, this just might prove too obvious to someone when they found wires strung across the landscape to a location I preferred to keep secret.

Another item I have included in my scheme of things is foraging. I had not necessarily planned on relying on it as strongly as the coming events dictate. It is a most useful and practical bit of know how for my well being. I would strongly recommend a foraging book, suited for your area, be included in your library. It will prove to be fun, educational, nutritional and necessary if circumstances degrade to the point of your having to survive from foraging from the land.

There are plants with edible leaves, some with edible roots, and many with edible fruits. Time will not allow you the option of observing animals to find suitable foods. Besides, animal often have special ways to deal with toxin in foods that we would find deadly. You can find berries that will delight the palate, and nuts that may be new to you but are just as good, maybe even better than those you can purchase at the grocery store. There will be a variety of mushrooms that any gourmet cook would be envious. Careful with mushrooms, many look similar, so look twice and then again with a very good photo likeness or better still, get an experienced forager to teach you the difference. Get a very good book.

I am sure there are many who would and could successfully add to the various projects I have written about. In more favorable times, I would possibly included some aquiculture, a pig or two foraging for themselves, and the planting of grape canes and blackberry in places over the land that would support them, and from which I could later harvest. These are not favorable times.

Chapter 16

IRAQ

Scholars generally agree on three basic premises concerning Iraq. Premise one is that Iraq is probably the location of the biblical Garden of Eden. Premise two is that Iraq was probably the cradle of modern civilization. The third premise, concerning Iraq, is that Iraq will not be one of the Arab nations that attack Israel as predicted in the Holy Bible. I ask myself then, "what role will Iraq play on the world stage and why write a chapter about them?". It is my conclusion from observing world events that Iraq's role, though secondary in nature, will be that of a catalyst in bringing about the final wars.

Iraq has often been estranged from the rest of the Arab world and has caused much embarrassment to them. At one time, they were the pride of the Arab nations, for within its borders lay the fabled city of Babylon. The talk of the then known world for her beauty and almost mythical "Hanging Gardens". Iraq brought to the civilized world a level of knowledge in mathematics and astronomy, never seen nor dreamed. They gave the world a working calendar of such accuracy, modern science can improve upon it only slightly. For it's time, Iraq was considerably ahead of men of other nations. Whether you want to coincide her fall from greatness with the fall of Babylon is your call, but for me, that is when the God of Israel damned Iraq.

Iraq became a nation fallen from unparalleled glory. Never again in the centuries that followed, did she come near reclaiming her pride and glory. It was as if she had vanished and just swayed to and fro as other nations came into prominence and fell to be replaced by other nations. In fact, the Arab nations as a whole seem to go dormant and the world stage shifted westward. Arabia became the land of romantic tales of flying carpets, mystical genies, heroic thieves and heros of literature like "Lawrence of Arabia" and the "Charge of the Light Brigade" until after the Second World War.

The great event that drew the world's attention back to Arabia was the struggle and success of Israel establishing a foot hold on what was considered Arab soil. The ensuing wars and confrontations between the struggling nation of Israel and the opposing Arab countries kept world attention drawn toward the region. Still, to the Arab mind, this question of rightness or ownership is not over.

Another important event that drew the attention of the world back to Arabia was the discovery of vast quantities of oil reserves in the region. Such riches were desired by the oil hungry industrial nations who waged an industrial war in attempting to be the primary recipient of this oil and the resulting political influence in these backward and under developed countries. As these oil reserves were developed, the new found financial wealth was first hoarded by the previous tribe leaders. Once gluttony sat in, then and only then, did the leaders begin building the infrastructure of a modern society. The peoples began reaping some of the benefit of this wealth but more significantly, the government possess the financial means to combat their sworn enemy, Israel.

Iraq, along with the other Arab nations, was thwarted time and again by what appeared a smaller and less equipped Israel nation. The United States support of Israel incensed Iraq against Israel's ally and against Iran who was very friendly to the United States. Iraq found a new leader who epitomized the feelings of the Iraqi peoples in Saddam Hussein. She needed little encouragement to take her fury out on her fellow Arab nation and Saddam's hidden agenda to reclaim Iraqi's rightful role of the leader of Arabia. While other Arab nations began taking a less focal and vocal position, Iraq seemed to scream louder.

Iraq lost to Iran but launched another attack over disputed land boundaries with Kuwait. Calculated as a reasonable risk, perhaps even thinking the rest of the world would just sit back and watch, Iraq swept into Kuwait as if its actions would cause no retaliation. For the first time in history, Arabia united along with the western powers to confront Iraq, militarily. Iraq was pushed back and severally punished for it's transgressions.

Having suffered seven years of embargos, Iraq continued to defy the world order. Apparently, she continued to develop bombs of mass destruction and to challenge the rights of the United Nations' inspection of her weaponry. So the stage was being set for Iraq to take it's role of being the catalyst of future world events. Dessert Fox, as the conflict of late 1998 was called, separated the ranks of the world coalition of 1991. When the United States and Great Briton took it upon themselves to be the policemen of world affairs, Iraq won a major victory. Most European, Russia, Japan, and most Arab countries cried out against the keepers of peace. While not quite siding with Iraq, there was no doubt that they were opposed to the actions of the United States and Great Briton.

The military embarrassment Iraq suffered during Dessert Fox cannot be compared with the triumphant victory she will experience during the consequently glorious role she will play among Arab nations in the future. This will provide for her the honor of being the Arabia spokesman against the infidels of the west. Iraq will boldly speak words the others fear to openly say, at least silent for a time. Iraq

will incite or attempt to incite war and terrorism against the western powers, and against Israel. She will continue to lay claim to disputed lands with Kuwait. She will still produce weapons of mass destruction. And when the day comes, when the biblical prophecy is fulfilled by Israel and the Dome of the Rock is removed from the site of Jerusalem's Holy Temple, she will call for an all out condemnation and apocalypse of Israel. Iraq is the trigger that unleashes the fury of Arabia.

Chapter 17

HIDEAWAY OCCUPIED

It was late afternoon, I ask myself "Why now, why this particular afternoon?". Lugging box after box into my hideaway cave, I pondered the question and was not finding an easy answer. It was a sixth sense or something like one that seemed to set off an alarm in my head and said, "Now is the time".

After almost two years of living in my reasonably small cottage or cabin, depending on one's taste, I had grown accustom to tight quarters. I had even, on occasions, spent a night or two in the cave just to get acquainted with its idiosyncratic nature. Even so, it was obvious in moments that I was not fully prepared for the restriction imposed by these two very small rooms, two spaces. The planning of this space had been fun, even exciting but you could only do so much.

Knowing that one day I just might have to truly live in my cave home, I had planned very carefully. Advantage had to be taken of the space of every nock and cranny. This very valuable space had to be put to its optimal usage, and looking around, it would seem that this requirement had been fulfilled. Yet, I was beginning to feel claustrophobic. I realized it was just the suddenness of the move, or what at that moment seemed a suddenness. Had I not planned for this event for over two years?

How much time would I have to spend in the cave "home"? I did not know. Regardless of the time, I had to get control immediately of my emotions, my fear. I worked harder, storing my clothes here, other supplies there, everything in its rightful place. I put the 410 shotgun and its 500 rounds in its recess within the door frame and closed the fascia board. I did the same on the opposite side of the doorway with the 22 rifle and 1000 rounds of long rifle cartridges. I thought I had been so clever to come up with such concealed compartments. Late that night I had all my "stuff" stowed away, at least as best I could. I walked outside.

Nothing was going on untoward, at least, and I was tired, but too keyed up to relax. I stood in the darkness listening, gazing at the stars, and even said a small prayer of thankfulness for my safety and for this new home of mine. It was so peaceful here in this backdrop of a mountain bluff, so delusional. One could almost forget the reason for my presence, the events that lead to this moment of time.

I had watched the year 2000 quietly roll in, and strangely enough the world did not stop spinning. Sure there was an alarm here and another there but nothing that at the moment seem to justify my predicted disasters. But as I watched, the year matured, and as it did the world seem to take on a life of its own. Nations, small ones at first, began to crumble, and the slumping stock markets of the world began to seem a little frayed. The news media would report these events as if they were occurring in another galaxy, a different earth than ours. People were not panicking, nor were business men jumping out windows. Normality seemed to be every where, yet, nations and the world economies were slowly but assuredly failing. I recall the very first true signs, in my opinion, that occurred were those events being reported in and around major European cities.

The Euro currency had started with a bang, a great success. First the banks had adopted this all new medium of exchange, and within a year, the public had been allowed to partake. You could go to Italy, or say Germany, and pull out enough Euro dollars and buy anything. For a European, it was like we Americans have done since our beginning, they would cross over into another country, not worry about the exchange. They purchased what they desired, until.

There was the report from Hungary, about a German coming into town and attempting to purchase a truck load of food items. His Euro currency was turned down. As reported, the proprietor tried to explain to the German, that it was not the money but that his regular customers had first claim on the food. "But," said the German, "You have always sold me these goods and have taken Euro dollars for them." "My business depends on our being able to purchase these goods." "I am sorry Herr Snyder, my government demands that any food items merchant have must be sold to the peoples of Hungary, first." "I cannot help you." Just a human interest story far away across the Atlantic.

Rome news media reported an increase in street vandalism. Every large city probably has its homeless or bag ladies and its vandalism. Why was this little story of any interest for world distribution. "The vandals seem to be concentrating on obtaining food items which could be sold on the black market", so the article stated. I noticed that it was not reported to be special food items, just food items. Was there a shortage of "food items" in Rome? I remembered the story from Hungary, was there a shortage of "food items" there also?

I found it interesting when one day it was reported that almost a complete crop of grapes had been harvested from a vineyard in the Rochelle province of France. Seems the thieves had simply waited until darkness, off loaded a small army of pickers with their baskets and drove away with a large truck load of grapes. I had never heard of anything like it. Not being in the grape business, I really didn't think this was a very wise move on the part of the thieves. Who would buy the grapes soon enough before they spoiled, I asked? Several days later, a follow up story appeared stating that the thieves had been found but not the grapes. The perpetrators of this bazaar theft explained it this way. They would steal the grapes, haul them to a certain location at which they would turn over the truck and its load to others "in exchange for food items". It was like the old axiom, "I digga the ditch, to get the money, to buy the food, to get the strength, to digga the ditch." But in this case, they stole the grapes for the food.

South Africa was in turmoil. Back in the early part of 1999, the black farmers were compensated, either with money or the return of their ancestral land, for the lands taken from them years prior. On the surface, the decision for this action seemed appropriate. It appeared the return of tribal lands was fair and honorable . Much of these lands had been developed into subdivisions, shopping centers and such and when the government, under world pressure, began to include these developed lands in the settlement with the tribes, things worsened. Civil war broke out, blacks killing whites, whites killing blacks and year 2000 slowly was passing on into the year 2001. Farms had been neglected, food was becoming scarce and still tempers flared. The war seemed to be taking on a new tenure. People were killing others, even their own, for a morsel of food.

Slowly, very slowly the bubble of economic splendor was leaking. Its brilliant sheen was fading and the dreaded predictions of Y2K impact upon the world was coming true. My only solace was that this madness, Thank God, had not reached my country. It is so easy to be lulled into a sense of safety. This comforting feeling was mine until about six months ago.

The day's effort had left me exhausted and my retreat into the night under the stars had not expelled this weariness of body, nor of the soul. I still did not have my answer as to the timing of my move, but I did not want to think any more. I just wanted to sleep.

Morning seemed to come extra early. I was not completely rested, but there were still many things that had to be done. I used trail number two and went back to my sports utility van. From a vantage point just about 500 yards from the cave, I could sit and observe the cottage. Everything seemed the same as when I left the day before. There were a few other items I wanted for the upcoming days and of course, they were at the cabin. So with caution, I let the van roll down the slight incline. Not starting the engine was another precaution, noises would draw attention, and that was the very last thing I wanted. It was hard enough to use different paths to and from the cave, and I surely did not want to alert someone of my presence.

Everything seemed to be okay in and about the cabin. The work shop was secure and none of the raised bed vegetables disturbed. These would have to be harvested soon or they would rot in place. I had more than enough stored in the root cellar, canned and fresh. Losing these few late maturing vegetables would cause me no concerned, but it was my nature to hate seeing waste. Lord knows, I had shared with my neighbors until they almost hated to see me drive up to their house. I guess I was the area's joke, all my fuss over the world economy, the continued break down of moral fiber becoming evident in our cities and my pseudo isolationist attitude.

After the first year of having bought this beautiful place, and having built the cabin and workshop, I quit inviting people over, even very close friends. I would go to their place, I would stop to talk to them, and of course, vegetables and fruits were delivered to others, often. Many times I tried to explain this behavior to myself, I really didn't think I was being paranoid, just intelligently cautious. So I said. The real reason, at least the most plausible one to me, was I reasoned that the least anyone knew about what I was doing, or the things I was building up by the bluff, the better.

About mid day, I had loaded the van with the tools I would need later, I had turned off the bottled gas, turned the electrical power switch to off, released the chickens to their own devices and released all the pigeons. I knew at that moment, that my life was truly changing, I would never see this labor of love in the same loving way. I had done all I could to protect what I had but now it must be in the hands of others.

I drove back to the area where I would park and hide the van. Again, as usual, I took a different route. I had learned long ago that trails are developed by repeated usage, caused by the continued compacting of the soil and disturbance of the surface. I did not want a trail to my van nor to either of the caves. The small trace of my drive would be almost gone after the first rain. After several, even a good Indian scout would have trouble finding my van.

Well, I have set up house so to speak and now the long wait began. During the sunlight hours I could keep up with the world using a solar powered radio. Thank goodness for a little music along the way too. The news continued to report the chaos in our larger cities as the result of fuel shortages and the resulting inability of trucking firms to bring in needed food supplies. Food store shelves were becoming more and more bare. These same stores were being looted of what food items they had.

Six months ago it had started. America had long been considered the food basket of the world. With fuel shortages, it could no longer produce foods in the same volumes as before. More significantly, it could not transport the available foods to locations of greatest need. As in the period of the "great depression", those in the cities were the first to feel the pinch of scarce food supplies.

Unlike those that lived through that experience, many of our society lacked the moral fiber to cope, so they stole what they needed. No soup lines for them.

Stories were being reported almost daily of mobs breaking into food stores and looting, neighbors fighting over a few canned goods, and even killing one another over food. I do not fear a rational man, but when a man watches his family starve, he often becomes irrational. We are witnessing a nation, at least in the cities, of men becoming irrational.

Our first local area incident occurred in a small community about thirty miles away. Harrison, Arkansas is a town of about 10,000 people and is surrounded by families who grow some of their own foods. Even within the town, there are those who may raise a few chickens, have a garden and have small fruit orchards. It has always been a quiet community where neighbors helped neighbors. When the food became scarce and even the local farmers could not help, men became irrational. They would steal vegetables out of a neighbors garden. The same neighbor who had been sharing his bounty for years. Stores here were also being broken into for any food items in stock. It didn't take long before this quiet, peaceful town was up in arms.

Cattlemen and farmers in the surrounding areas began losing stock. The chicken industry of the area began losing chickens at night at an alarming rates. Pigs would mysteriously disappear in the middle of the night. Law enforcement were at a lose as to how to combat this escalating epidemic of crime. It wasn't long before gardens were being harvested by unknowns and smokehouses and root cellars were being striped of all their content.

Reviewing these events, while sitting in my cave, I found the answer to my question of "Why move now?". I had

drawn a mental chart of the progression of these events. It was obvious that the vandals were reaching further and further afield. They were coming my way and I had concluded that it would not be long in its coming. I had made the move because I had to. The thieves had struck a friend of mine who lived just 5 miles away. He had been awakened by the noise and had charged outside, gun in hand. In the ensuing conflict, he had been hurt, four of his cows had been stolen, five pigs, and the total content of his smokehouse. Fortunately for him, he had not been killed, none of his family were injured and they had not found his other root cellar with all his canned goods. After assisting him in every way I could, I returned home. In two more days, I made my move to, what I hoped to be, safety.

CHAPTER 18

FORAGING

Three days after my move to the hideaway, the thieves struck my place. As a last precaution, I had refused to lock the doors to my cabin. It was my hope that should the thieves come, they would take what little I had left and leave the cabin unharmed. The same was true concerning my workshop. I have to admit that leaving the workshop unlocked was a much harder decision. So they came, and took what they wanted in the way of food and all the small power tools from the workshop.

I walked down to the cabin to inspect the place. No damage to either structure. It was truly a relief but never the less I was angry and frustrated. I remembered the years it had taken me before I could afford all the fine electrical tools now gone. One should count his blessings and remember that things could be replaced. I found little comfort in this thought but I was truly thankful for life. Some day, the tools would be and could be replaced.

Not for a moment did I believe the thieves would not return. My daily routines were done remembering this possibility, always. I never came to the cabin without first sitting quietly in a hidden spot observing what might be going on near by and down at the cabin. At no time would I use the same trail twice in a row. Seldom did I actually need to go to the cabin, but I found comfort in being there, hoping one day to return in peace.

I was very careful not to overburden my supplies, either of food or fuel. I had plenty of food stored either fresh or canned.

As for as fuel, I had stored six bottles of bottled gas for cooking. In the mean time, I could often use a solar oven to cook most foods. This simple device I had first seen while surfing on the Internet. It was simply a box within a box, insulated in between. The inside box was lined with aluminum foil and the lid was a piece of sheet glass. All you had to do was place it on a slant with the glass top facing the sun. The temperature inside would reach 350 degrees if you rotated the oven to always be facing the full sun. A smokeless and reusable means of cooking.

As for conserving my food supply, I began foraging. I had acquired several books on the subject earlier and had done some practice over the first two years prior to my move to the hideaway. I was always amazed at the variety of foods I could forage, although not all of it was as tasty as I would prefer. Now, I had to forage for survival.

One of the first things I did before starting to forage, was to make sure the planting beds I had prepared two years ago were planted with seasonal and appropriate seeds. The seeds I used were not hybrid which meant I could use seeds from the resulting fruit as my seeds for the next season of planting. From this harvest I could expect peas, beans, squash, melons, greens of all sorts, garlic, onion, potatoes, yams, and if I was lucky, peanuts and tomatoes. In a very isolated area I had planted popcorn and regular field corn. I new I would have very strong competition from all the wildlife for these but hoped I would at least get a small share.

Foraging is simply finding food items which are safe to eat, being sure to recognize the safe ones from the unsafe ones, gathering the items found and learning how to prepare them. I had grown up in the south where pokeweed flourished and was familiar with the preparation of these wonderful greens. I already new that the fruit and roots were poisonous so they were no problem.

I had used wild onions many times to prepare game I had killed while on hunting trips. I was already aware of the benefit of eating the base portion of cattail plants but there were non in my immediate area. What I needed to find were the plants and fruits in my current location for I did not have the luxury of traveling around in the nearby country side.

One of the hardest items to identify as far as safety were the edible mushrooms. These fungi are very nourishing but can be very deadly. I would walk around by the bluff, or into the woods and on the edges of the little grass land of my farm. I always carried my book on mushrooms with me when going afield. I would compare the pictures with the live specimen, check to see if it had a collar or not. When satisfied it was safe, I would harvest each type, place each type in its separate bag before returning home. After I arrived at the cave, I would repeat the ritual of precaution, examining each type again against the book. If again I was satisfied, I would dry each specie separately, store in tight sealed plastic bags. At first, I went through an additional test. I would prepare a very tiny sample and eat it. If I did not die, I knew it was safe. I have to admit this last test was not really on the bright side and consider myself very lucky.

Fruits and nuts were the easiest items to forage. Over the years I had become familiar with dewberries, blackberries, muscadine, other wild grapes, wild pecan, walnuts and hickory nuts. I had also planted in various spots cultivar blackberries and blue berries. My orchard was still intact so, in season, I had those fruits to forage. I use the word forage for I would still be competing with the potential thieves. Another food source would be the flowers of certain plants. I had sucked the nectar from honeysuckle flowers many times as a kid and would soon learn the other wild flowers that could be eaten.

When a kid visiting my country cousins, they would play tricks on me, their city cousin. While walking along their pasture fences, they would bend over and pick the fruit of a certain low growing plant. They would eat the seed and maybe give me a taste. The object was for me to like the seed and want more. Of course, they would simply bend over another plant, pick the fruit, eat the seed and walk on. It didn't take me long to realize that they were not going to share and if I wanted more I would have to pick my own. To my chagrin, the plant was bull nettle and I am afraid I was not as cautious as they. This little plant's leaves and stem are covered with little hairy projections and when rubbed against cause a terrible itch. I learned my lesson but had to pay the cost.

Another very unpleasant lesson came when I was introduced to a green persimmon. The same cousins. When you bite into a green persimmon, your mouth seems to draw up like you had just eaten alum. Most unpleasant for the victim but hilarious to the on lookers. Both lessons were useful now that I had to forage.

I have always enjoyed hunting and would never kill an animal just for the "sport" of it. If I did not plan to eat it, I would not kill it. I still feel that way but now I did not hunt, I foraged. A fresh killed rabbit or squirrel prepared with wild mushrooms and wild onions taste mighty good and are small enough to eat in one day. I would use my 22 rifle or my 410 shotgun to harvest these critters. My firearms were too small caliber for deer, besides, a deer was too large an animal for quick consumption. Occasionally, I took a mourning dove, or duck when I could get up close. The duck would be a meal but I had to get several dove to make one. If I was lucky, I would jump a covey of quail. Oh!, these were fine eating.

Roaming the woodlands, as I did, it wasn't long before I found a wild bee hive. This was such a lucky break and fortunately for me, I had planned for this event many months prior. When I found my first hive, I marked it so I could find it again. I would return to the cave and gather the necessary tools and items I knew I would need.

My plan was to return to the hive the following day and begin preparing the hive for continuous harvest of the honey cones. Wild bee hives are often made in the hollow of a very large limb and some times in the hollow of a tree trunk. Tree trunks were usually too large to do what I had planned.

At the hive, I would make a horizontal saw cut about six inches above the entry hole. I would also make a horizontal cut about six inches below the entry hole. This was done late in the afternoon when most of the bees were at home and I could plug the entry hole. This is all I would do the first evening. On the second night, if the bees were not still disturbed by my sawing, I would do step two. If they appeared to be disturbed, I would wait one night for step two.

Step two was to separate my sawed portion from the rest of the limb. What I was aiming for was my ability to use a chisel and small maul to split the cut portion from the remaining portion of the limb. Usually a few strong taps on the wood from saw cut edge to saw cut edge, vertically, would separate this wood slab. When successful, I would take a piece of rope and tie it back in place. If I disturbed the bees too much, they might swarm and I would lose my hive of bees.

Again, on the following evening, I would observe the activities of the bees. If not too disturbed, I would attach two hinges on one side of this split out section. On the opposite side, I would attach a handle. Now I had created the equivalent of a door. I would wait a full week before trying the door or harvesting a portion of the honey cone.

After my wait of one week, I would return to the hive and watch for bee activities. I always did this after first light which would give the worker bees time to be out foraging for nectar and pollen. I certainly did not want to open a bee hive full of agitated bees. If all went well, I would blow smoke into the entry hole, and gradually pry open the door. As the door began to open I would blow smoke into the resulting crack. Why smoke calms bees I don't know but it does. Now with the door opened, I use a knife and slice one large cone from the rest of the cones, causing as little damage to the remainder as possible. When I use this honey, I now just have to return, blow smoke and harvest. This approach works most of the time for me.

Living off the land is fun, if not always filling. Of all the things I have had to do during my isolation period, I believe foraging has aided in my keeping my sanity. It is a time consuming task and can be very educational.

CHAPTER 19

HUNTING SEASON

The morning air was very crisp and there was a feel in the weather that only impending snow storms bring. The hunting season had been legally opened for several months now and the hunting in this area is always very good. I had been able to provide all the meat I wanted and needed without creating much disturbance. The little 410 shot gun barely makes enough noise to be heard from afar and the 22 rifle even quieter. It was during these reflective times I was very pleased with myself in having made such logical choices in weapons. But my enemy would be the snow.

Until now, I could go and come, always using different paths and could easily do a little hunting while keeping an eye open for edible plant life. Since I used different routes, I wasn't concerned that someone just might cross my path and follow me back to my caves. When it snowed, and it would certainly snow, my passing through the woods would leave telltale signs.

My neck of the woodland area of Arkansas is one of the prized areas for hunting. Elk had been introduced back into the state several years ago, and though I have never seen elk in the wild, its introduction and eventual permit hunting had served as an advertizement to hunters from all over the state. They had come for the elk, stayed for the other game and returned often.

There are many little homesteads scattered around our region. This has provided wonderful areas for the several game birds who have taken advantage of the open spaces between woodlots. Rabbits, too, like the fence rows and the fresh green-eries we homesteaders plant year after year. It is almost impossible to prevent bramble from growing up into the fences and rabbits feel safer among them. An occasional covey of quail can be flushed from these same bramble piles and in some tightly controlled area, even a pheasant. The pheasant has not adapted to our area very well.

Seems these transition areas between woodland and pasture or crop land has encouraged the mourning dove as well. They like the low shrub growth to make their nest and if it is close to a water source, they like it even better. I have never seen a dove in thick woodland.

About eighty five percent of our woodland is comprised of hardwoods, most of which is oak. While a person might find a squirrel in pine forest, when given a choice, the squirrel prefers a breakfast, lunch and dinner of acorns. The squirrel is probably the most plentiful of our game animals and I have had great luck in providing meat for the table using squirrels. But when the snow comes, things will get tougher.

I had never had to spend a winter in the woods, hunting and foraging for food before. The shortage of food and the shortage of fuel for vehicles just might be enough to keep the non resident hunter from this part of the world. I just did not know, but one thing was certain, when it snowed, I would have to be extra careful with my trails. A person never really knows what else is in the woods with him. I have been standing still watching for squirrel movement in the tree tops and had other hunters walk within fifteen or twenty yards of my spot and never know I was there.

It was two weeks before it snowed. It had started very light at about eight o'clock at night. I sat watching it in the moonlight and hoped this would remain light and melt in about two or three days. The next morning, the snow was still falling, but this time, it was not light, it was coming down in flurries. Snow was building up in the trees and upon the ground very quickly. If you walked out upon the snow, the tracks were very obvious. The temperature had fallen, and that meant the snow would not be a quick melt as I had hoped.

Several days passed before I felt I just had to venture out into the snow. During that time, I had not heard any evidence of hunters in the woods. That, of course, did not mean they were not there, or had not been there. Easier places existed for the initial hunt of game and most hunters prefer these areas when the game was plentiful. Then there was the problem of fuel shortage. No one was going to use up their supply of gas any faster by going a greater distance for game, especially when there was plenty close at hand.

So I ventured out. Very cautiously at first, especially until I got some distance from me and the hideaway cave. I took every precaution I had ever read about in concealing my trail. When you have to do this, progress toward your destination is slow. As an added precaution, I had decided that I would always go prepared to spend the night outdoors. My preacher brother had once told me of the precautions people from the northeast of the United States took when going out driving from place to place. They never knew when they might get stuck in a snow storm so they always had an extra supply of warm cloths, blankets, snow chains and if they were smart, a flashlight and some food. This seemed good advise in my current circumstances except the chains

The first place I wanted to go was to my observation bluff. From there I could observe any activity going on, or in this case, any fresh tracks in and around the place. There are several ways to get to my woodland area and the adjoining government property but the most logical would be by using my roadway to my cabin. In this situation, the snow was my ally. If anyone had been stirring around after the snow had fallen, they too would leave tracks.

Snow scenes found on a postcard is the best way I can describe the view. The only thing missing was the curl of smoke coming from the chimney. No tracks, no one invading my homestead, no need to be angry or feel unsafe. I was pleased but it is still hard to face the uncertainty of the days ahead. They were not there today, but just as surely that the snow would fall, so would their return.

Hunting was very good this first hunt in the snow. Now, I know to some this would not be considered much of a hunt. I only got two very fine red fox squirrels and a young rabbit. To me, this meant I would not have to hunt for meat for three days, three days of not making and hiding tracks. These were bad times. People were going hungry and would think nothing of stealing what little bit I had just to have food. I realize that I am isolated from most of this madness and relatively safe from hungry encroachers. But I have had one invasion into my residence and a neighbor almost killed. That was several months ago. I mustn't let myself drop my guard for if they found me, they might force me to reveal my root cellar and hideaway. Even if they left me alone afterwards, I would be hard pressed to survive just off the land.

While already out, I decided to pass by the root cellar cave on my way back to the hideaway. An onion, or a sweet potato, just about anything different would taste awfully good with this meat. That is one thing you miss when living off the land, variety. I love to cook and had never had to do without any spice or dish that would be the perfect compliment to a main course. So going to the cellar was like a luxury. Up until this time, I had not had to go very often for there was plenty variety found in my foraging for plants. With the snow on the ground, this would be increasingly difficult.

Everything at the cellar was safe and in good order. It was good to know it was there and it was good to be back in the hideaway. It will get cold in this cave during the day and I had to wear extra cloths but it was home. At night, I could build a fire and let the smoke drift up through a stovepipe chimney. The fire had to be small but so was the space it had to warm. I looked forward to these moments of peace and quiet and the warmth of my little fire. There was no breeze to whip the smoke around or to dissipate the heat too quickly. So I burned small pieces of wood until the space was nice and cozy. At first lighting of the fire, I often had enough light to read by, but I seldom did any reading. I also had plenty of daylight hours to read by but when its cold outside, the fire made a nice reading light.

Things remained relatively calm and safe during this first phase of snowfall, snow melt and then a new snowfall. A more or less typical pattern of weather in this part of the country. Snow came again during the second week of January, and this snow was going to stay for a long visit. Its friends, more snow falls, would join it until early Spring before it would slowly melt away.

I awakened one cold morning to the sound of gunshot. It wasn't close or at least it did not seem to be close considering my being enclosed in a cave. Like a muffled sound, but loud enough to give me a start. I quickly dressed and gathered my overnight survival pack. Poking my head out, like I was the thief or intruder, I listened for more blast. If I heard another, perhaps I could detect the direction of the blast and the closeness of the hunter. It was slow waiting. I had spent enough time hunting over the years to know that what I heard had been a heavy gauged shotgun, probably a twelve. I also knew that if the hunter was hunting for deer, that he would probably have used two shots. Deer fever does that to a hunter, the first shot often kills the game but the adrenaline is flowing and you just have to take that second shot. There was but the one shot.

A one shot suggest two possibilities to me. Skilled and experienced hunters do not waste extra shots. They have overcome the effect of buck fever through time and experience. The other possibility would be a squirrel or rabbit hunter. A twelve gauge shotgun is mighty heavy armor for these small creatures unless a person was hoping for a deer but would take any game. Food was food. It was not the time in world affairs to be a sportsman. You killed what ever could be put on the table for your family to eat.

Another telltale sign about small game hunters was the fact you seldom saw two animals together. Even if you did, it is always better to concentrate on one, getting the best shot and kill on the one shot rather than lose both animals. So, having shot the one, you would often wait for the second squirrel to move before shooting the second time. Had it been an isolated animal, the hunter slowly moves on to the next promising spot. His shooting would be a sign to those listening as to the type hunting he was up to.

The second shot had not come. So for a while, I would be in the dark as to what game was being hunted and the hunters relative location. Waiting like this is hard work. You have your own flow of adrenaline and no answers. I dare not move from the entrance of the cave until I knew the location of the hunter. Then again, there was no guarantee that only one hunter was out. I had to hear at least one before I would move. Chances were that the hunters, if there were more than one, would be in the same general area. Then I could make some sort of investigation. Three hours passed and no sound. Their hunt and mine was over for the day.

The next day I left the cave and made a wide circle around its perimeter. I knew I would not likely find hunters but I surely would find tracks. If I could cut the hunter's tracks, I could trail them to a possible kill site. I hoped what I would find, if I found anything, would be the evidence of a deer kill. A deer would provide a lot of meat, and the hunter would have little need for a quick return. In about two hours I had found the hunter's trail. He was moving away from my cave but had apparently been too close for my comfort. At the end, I found the field dress remains of a large deer and the trail leading away was away from me and mine.

It was cold, and the sounds from the outside had been quiet. I needed to be doing something so decided it was safe to venture out. Grabbing my survival pack, I sat out for my observation bluff . Moving away from the cave and in a different direction of the bluff, I slowly made my way, covering my trail the best I could. In around about way, I arrived at the bluff. The first thing I saw was evidence that someone had paid me a visit at the cabin. Smoke was curling up out of the chimney. Whoever it was, possibly the hunter, had decided to take up residence in my homestead for awhile. Oh!, you don't know how angry that made me. I would have given anything I had for the asking, but for some one to take from me always stirred such anger in me.

I felt so helpless. There was no way I could safely confront these intruders. I had worked too hard to put all this into jeopardy. For once in my life, I had to sit back and take it. The consoling factor was that at least I knew the where about of the hunter. I could watch his comings and goings and that would give me a sort of power over him.

It wasn't long before my vigilance was rewarded with a glimpse of my house guest. A tall lanky fellow came strolling out of the cabin, like he owned the place and went to a camper truck.

The kind of camper you just shove into the back of a pickup. He got something out of the camper and went back to the warmth of the cabin. There he was sitting in my cabin, warm and probably eating venison and here I sat cold and chewing on jerky. More anger.

Within about an hour another person emerged from the cabin, going to the camper. It appeared to be a young boy but could have been a girl in pants. Which ever it was didn't matter, what did matter is that it could mean that a family had moved into my cabin. What in the world possessed other folks to feel like they could just move into another man's home and treat it as if it was their due. I answered my own question, a family disparate because the world has gone crazy and like so many in the great depression, they have lost everything, even their pride. I reminded myself that it was not rational men I had to fear, but irrational men driven to despair due to circumstance beyond their control or understanding. My anger lessened. I could not help them, but I would do nothing to hurt them, either.

This family was the first to find refuge in my cabin, they left things neat and tidy as they had found them. They apparently stole nothing other than the warmth and comfort of my cabin. For this I am truly thankful and a little proud that I had built a sturdy place that could be shared, even with intruders. Several times more was my cabin turned into a place of refuge. I found hunters and would be hunters in the woods. I heard them fire their arms and hoped they had gotten their family a little food. I wanted them to make it, I wanted the time to be short so that all of us could return to a world of normalcy.

For two hard years now, I have watched them come and go. Each time they had come in peace and left in peace. Only once, only one visitor had come in hatred or destruction. No, I am not

talking about the ones who came during the first month of isolation. They came and took, but they did not destroy.

The destroyer came angry, at himself, at the world, at his inability to provide food for his family. I trailed him several days as
he attempted to understand the world of the hunter. Oh, he had a
gun, and he could shoot it, he just could not find game. Had he
found it, I am not sure he could properly use his gun, but he could
shoot it. He would do nearly everything imaginable wrong. He
stomped around in the woods like animals had no ears. He would
swing out at this and that, cursing the whole time, sometimes as
loud as he could. His cursing was at everything, and everybody,
even God. With this one, I almost broke my rule of not interfer-
ing. The man was in such need and his family so hungry, it almost
tore my heart out. But no, this man could not be trusted. The
kind that would bite the hand that feed him and laugh in your face.
No, I would not help him.

After several frustrating days, the man and his family moved
on. To where, I never found out, but I won't forget him. He was
a man of destruction, a man of frustrations and a man of desperation. Out of anger or meanness, this man burned my cabin. I
would like to think that it was a mistake, but later I found evidence that it was arson. The cabin can be rebuilt, but this man's
soul will be scarred forever.

**The burning of the cabin ended the days I had visitors.
Soon, the crazy world would turn itself around, I could rebuild my cabin and I would be able to go home. I have
suffered much during these two years, I have watched as
others suffered, but I know that I have survived the worst,
this time.**

Chapter 20

THE ORDEAL

The year is 2005, late fall and all is at peace. At peace in my little world. From the news I can gather, it would seem the worst of the ordeal of the last five years has come to an end, men are looking again toward the future not their next meal. It has been a bitter experience and struggle to survive under such adverse conditions, I wonder if man has learned anything of import.

My little world, the hideaway, my burned cabin, my root cellar and my life on the mountain knoll is just a miniature cosmos of the world as a whole. I have suffered exile from my home, I have been deprived of its sanctuary, its warmth and comfort. The intruders to my haven were like the military invaders of countries, the destroyer was my enemy. Rather than having to join the throngs of refugees, I roamed upon the earth alone, but like them, all I wanted was to survive this terrible ordeal that was not of my making. Yet, I was one of the very lucky ones, blessed in having the forethought to prepare for the chaos that permeated the minds and hearts of man.

London, Berlin, Paris, Tokyo, New York, New Orleans, Atlanta, Miami, San Francisco, and Los Angeles and oh so many more of our world's great cities were in shambles. Inconceivable is the amount of destruction mobs of hungry, frustrated people can wrought in their anger and great need. At first it was looting for looting's sake, then the riots and combat over the last of the food items. No store was safe, no home, for if the mob suspected food was present, every stone was turned, so to speak, to find it. Fights and killings were everywhere, to imagine all this over a scrap of food.

Prior to the end of 1999, the peoples of the world became concerned that perhaps the Y2K problem would have greater impact upon their lives than they had previously been told. Bank accounts had been withdrawn so they would have ready cash in hand, just in case the computer problems effected the bank. Money hoarded as if it were precious gold. Many felt prepared by stock-piling foods and water. Retailers experienced a boom if they were in the food business, but the others witnessed the staggering retail slump during the expected Christmas buying spree.

When the stock markets began plummeting in the early days of 2000, world leaders were always positive that these setbacks were temporary. I wondered how they could claim that it was temporary while on the same front page, banks were closing or failing all over the country. I suppose politicians have to remain politicians even as the world crumbles around their feet. They want the public to think that they alone have the answer, that a vote for them is a vote in the right direction.

This same theme was being viewed by the peoples world wide. Brazil had fallen, Mexico had fallen, Russia had fallen and short of a miracle Japan would soon fall. The domino effect was on a rampage. As one major industry closed its doors, so would a dozen more smaller companies close theirs. These small suppliers of the large conglomerate sometimes fell before the conglomerate. The effect is the same, big waves or little waves all cause erosion. And just assuredly as I am sitting here telling you my story, the financial world was eroding and was on a collision course with disaster.

The great destructive forces, the riots, the mobs didn't really start until food shortages were evident. When the fuel industries of the world became engulfed in the overall collapse of world economy, the farmer could no longer produce, the food shippers could not transport, and the local warehouses were quickly emptied. I have said this several times, but it bares repeating, we have nothing to fear from the rational man.

Men and their families became hungry and frustrated. It is a very small step from being rational to becoming irrational in such circumstances. The surge started in the large cities and as supplies were exhausted, spilled over into the country sides, leaving in their wake the shamble of cities and of lives. No one suspected of hoarding food was safe, unless they could not be found, as in my case.

One of the most interesting aspects of all that happened during this five year period was to realize that the people of the less developed counties fared the best. Even China, with it billions, saw little of the madness of the mob, with the exception of in some of her larger cities. Agrarian societies were able to cope for they could not afford the expensive agriculture machines which consumed fuels. What did they care if fuel was in short supply? Latin American's low income workers were use to scraping out a subsistence without the government's or industries' help. Neighbor had no need to steal from neighbor, food was shared with great abandonment just as was the perpetual poverty.

The industrialized, effluent countries of the world had grown away from the agrarian way of life. Even the United States, who was considered to be the bread basket of the world had evolved away from a farmer and rural society. In so doing, she had supported the incorporation of the bulk of her farmlands into the hands of giants of agriculture. She had removed the support fibers that allowed the family farms to exist. Through her misunderstanding, she had supported the giants while undercutting her own foundational base on which our great country was founded. The family farmer, often of many generations, and the small business man were under supported and over regulated, systematically.

In these last few weeks, I have had the opportunity to visit many of my neighbors of five years ago. Not one had fared nearly so well as I, but all had survived. They had survived because we live in an area that is reasonably isolated from the large city mobs. We survived because we are a people use to growing our own foods and sharing the abundance with the less fortunate. We as a whole survived because we as a community still believe in the Christian principles taught in our churches, that we are truly to "love our neighbor as our self." Many survived because their neighbor, as myself, would slip through the darkness of night to leave a basket of food at their doorstep. Sometimes it might be just a squirrel or rabbit or two, but what we did for one another came from a deeper respect of the goodness of man rather than the need for praise.

Many stories were told during our gatherings. We were all drawn together out of gratitude for our having been spared the blunt of the turmoil, because of the kindness of our neighbors and our strong desire to repay in kind. Not one of my neighbor friends had to stand alone. If he needed help to rebuild a barn, or in my case a cabin, hands were aplenty. Families were re-united who had to separate for one reason or another. Re-united not only with blood relatives but a community that cared about their well being.

New crops were planted from the few seeds that had survived the cook pot. Each neighbor gave of what he had of these precious bundles of life and those that did not get corn this year would receive ears from the harvest. No one had to worry about having all the type seeds he needed or wanted, each knew those that had would share in the bounty at harvest time. But the greatest seeds sown during these gatherings were the seeds of love. These seeds would grow over the years, drawing this small community even closer together, with the knowledge and assurance, that while part of this community, we would never truly be alone.

For the experiences these gatherings brought, the deep joy I felt over being a member of such a supportive community, I give thanks. They reminded me of my youth when a neighbor was a friend, and could be counted on. Those were good days, these were good days. Best of all, the ordeal was over.

About the Author

Born in north Louisiana, raised in south Arkansas where I learned to love nature, the hills and mountains. Educated in Music at Louisiana State University, with a minor in Science.

Thirty years in Data Processing, most of which was with State Government.

I have been a student of agriculture, nature, survival and human nature all my life. Some of it while in a formal course but most in observing and practicing what works. As an observer, I have seen the change from isolated country economies toward world dependent economies.

"Troubles on the Horizon" reflects my thoughts of what is about to happen. This is my first attempt at being a writer, but since its completion, I have a romantic novella to be published later this year, and three more works in the making.

In addition, I have a book of poems I hope to get published.